I0763321

MAGGS 52

Ghost of New York

Concept and story by

Barbara Williams and Mary Ann Giannino

Screenplay by

Richard T. Davidson

Cover Illustration by

Dana Biviano

Cover digitally remastered by

Philip Beska

Book formatting by

Vincent Bivona

This book is a work of fiction. Names, characters, places, and incidents either are products of the authors' imagination or are used fictitiously.

ISBN: 978-1-7351017-0-5

In Memoriam

To my beloved son, Tommy Giresi.

In life, you are my rock, my happiness, my everything.
We will always be connected through all of eternity.
Until we meet again in Heaven.

Love, Mom

To Michael Leili,

Thank you for always being there for me.
You were a good friend, not only to me, but to my son, Tommy.
God bless you, Mike.

Love, your friend, Barbara.

FADE IN:

EXT. NIGHTCLUB -- THE SHARK TANK -- NIGHT

SUPERIMPOSE ON SCREEN: MIAMI, FLORIDA - 2007

WE HEAR music.

WE SEE a huge line of PEOPLE stand in front of a popular nightclub called "*THE SHARK TANK.*"

WE MOVE inside.

INT. NIGHTCLUB -- -- THE SHARK TANK -- MOVING -- CONTINUOUS

The club is massed with PEOPLE. Hip. Hard Techno thumps. Very sexy. Very crowded.

WE MOVE through the busy nightclub and pass by all types of races, creeds, and colors.

WE STOP on the DANCE FLOOR.

ANGLE ON:

27-YEAR-OLD MAGGIE MAY O'BRIAN.

She is a white, Irish Catholic woman with long red hair. She wears a short, black skirt, black knee-high boots, and a little white tank top. Some freckles scatter about her face, giving life to her green eyes. Her petite 5'4" frame held together by a workout regimen of at least five days a week.

ANGLE ON:

A shiny, silver WATCH on her left wrist.

Even with a full Dance Floor of PEOPLE around her, she dances by herself.

A BLOND WOMAN named KATE parts through the crowded Dance Floor. She is hot and dressed to kill. She struts up to MAGGIE and leans in to her ear with a whisper.

MAGGIE takes her hand. The TWO exit the Dance Floor.

They MOVE towards a STAIRCASE in the rear of the club and begin to ascend the staircase. At the top of the staircase is a door. KATE opens the door with a key and walks inside.

Just before MAGGIE enters, she looks down towards the MAIN BAR on the far side of the club.

P.O.V. MAGGIE:

She eyes an AFRICAN AMERICAN man named GARY. He's six foot two, two hundred pounds. He gives MAGGIE a head nod.

He looks towards a SIDE BAR to his right and signals a short, stocky CAUCASIAN man named CHARLIE.

The TWO men immediately leave their respected areas and make stride towards the staircase.

MAGGIE enters.

INT. NIGHTCLUB AARON'S OFFICE CONTINUOUS

Inside the Office is club owner, AARON JACOBSEN. He sits behind a huge mahogany desk with a glass top.

The Office itself is sharp. A 80" flat screen hangs behind him on his eggshell white walls. A black leather couch hugs the wall to the left with two leather chairs in front of his desk. Black carpeting covers the floor.

AARON is five foot seven, two hundred and fifty pounds. He wears a black ARMANI suit. A red tie dangles loosely around his white undershirt. His head is down, ready to inhale a huge line of COCAINE. He sniffs it up his nose.

MAGGIE closes the door behind her. The loud Techno drowns out.

KATE

Hey there, Aaron.

(smiles)

You going share?

AARON looks up at KATE. His nose is red and his eyes are the size of saucers.

AARON
(sniffs)
Of course.
(beat)
Who's your friend?

KATE struts over and sits on AARON's lap. AARON cuts a line of coke for KATE.

KATE
This is my friend Courtney, the new girl I've been telling you about.
(looks at Maggie with hungry eyes)
She's looking for work.

AARON
And what type of work is she looking for?

KATE
(smiles)
Club work, silly.

Apparently MAGGIE is using an alias. She steps forward with confidence.

MAGGIE
Yeah! Club work, silly.

MAGGIE struts over to the couch and slowly crosses her legs. She mimics SHARON STONE from BASIC INSTINCT.

MAGGIE (CONT'D)
Do you have any openings?

AARON stares at MAGGIE's gorgeous legs.

AARON
(smiles)
So, Courtney, you think you can make me money on my floor?

KATE comes up from the desk with a huge sniff of cocaine. She licks her lips and fidgets with her nose.

KATE
She's smart and she's hot.
(sniffs)
The guys will eat her up.

MAGGIE
(smiles)
So will the girls.

KATE gets up off AARON's lap.

KATE
(to Aaron)
Thanks for the pick me up, baby.

She walks over and sits down next to MAGGIE on the couch. AARON takes a minute to size MAGGIE up.

AARON
How do I know you're not a cop?

MAGGIE
How do I know *you're* not a cop?

AARON tenses up from her sarcastic answer.

AARON
You think I'm playing games.
(shakes his head)
I have enough workers right now. Sorry, not hiring.
Get out!

MAGGIE thinks quickly. She has to change AARON's mind.

She quickly turns to KATE and forcefully kisses her. KATE responds by kissing her back. MAGGIE then starts to fondle KATE's breasts. She finally pulls away after about ten seconds. She stands up with a grin and fixes her lipstick on the side of her mouth.

She stares right at AARON, all business.

MAGGIE
I like a good hard drink, good pussy, and most of all,
I like money. And as you can tell, I am not a clock
puncher. The only overtime I want to do, is her . . .
(looks at Kate)
. . . after I make you and I some money tonight.

AARON smiles like a kid in a candy store. He stands up and walks over to MAGGIE. He eyes her up and down, down and up. He then grabs her "*ASS*" with a firm grip and holds it there.

AARON

I like you. You're full of surprises and attitude.

(beat)

Maybe I can join the two of you and show you a surprise of my own?

MAGGIE reaches down and smacks his hand away with authority.

MAGGIE

I'm a vegetarian.

(raises her eyebrows)

I don't do meat.

There's an awkward pause. We can tell AARON is not used to being told no.

MAGGIE (CONT'D)

(impatient)

So do I get the job or not?

AARON turns away from her and then swings wildly back around with a hard slap to MAGGIE's cheek.

MAGGIE crumbles to the floor from the unsuspecting blow.

AARON

(agitated)

You better think about changing your menu selection if you want to continue to work here.

MAGGIE is tough as nails. KATE sits frozen and nervous.

MAGGIE

Continue?

(beat)

Does that mean I'm hired?

KATE reaches down and helps MAGGIE to her feet. Her nose bleeds and her left cheek is noticeably swollen.

AARON walks over to his desk and rolls his chair out from under it. He then reaches into the top drawer of his desk and removes a clear REMOTE CONTROL.

He punches a "CODE" into the remote control.

ANGLE ON:

A BLACK SAFE ascends up from the floor from where his chair was. He punches another "CODE" into the remote control and the safe door opens automatically.

P.O.V. AARON:

Inside the safe are stacks of MONEY, A GUN, JEWELRY and all sorts of different NARCOTICS already bagged and separated.

AARON reaches inside and removes a BAG of white pills. He punches in another "CODE" and the safe closes and returns back into the floor, camouflaged with the carpet.

He tosses the BAG at MAGGIE's feet.

AARON
There are sixty pills in that bag.
(beat)
They're thirty dollars apiece. Bring me back eighteen Hundred dollars by the end of the week, no less.
(beat)
Then maybe we can work something out on a steady basis.

ANGLE ON:

MAGGIE sneakily slides her hand down her left wrist and pushes the side button on her WATCH.

CUT TO:

INT. NIGHTCLUB - MOMENTS LATER

GARY and CHARLIE look down at their WATCHES, which now blink RED. Instantly, they run up the staircase and draw GUNS.

INT. NIGHTCLUB -- OFFICE - MOMENTS LATER

The door swings open. GARY and CHARLIE enter, guns drawn.

CHARLIE
(aims at Aaron)
FREEZE. D-E-A! DON'T MOVE, ASSHOLE.

GARY rushes over and notices MAGGIE's nose bleed.

GARY
Are you all right, Maggie? Your nose is bleeding.

He hands her a handkerchief. MAGGIE takes it.

MAGGIE
(wipes her nose)
Thanks. I'm fine.

GARY reaches for an EARPIECE in his ear and pushes into a receiver.

GARY
(into receiver)
All clear. Suspect apprehended. Move in! Let's shut it down.

CHARLIE bends AARON across his desk and handcuffs him.

MAGGIE
Are you okay, Kate?

KATE
Yeah, I'm okay.
(looks at Aaron)
And I'm ready to put that piece of shit behind bars.

MAGGIE
Good. You'll get your chance.

AARON flips out. He realizes KATE has turned on him.

AARON
(shouts)
YOU BACK STABBING BITCH! YOU'RE FINISHED. I'LL HAVE YOU FUCKING KILLED FOR THIS!

MAGGIE walks over towards AARON vindictively. CHARLIE lifts AARON up off the desk.

MAGGIE

In the last six months three kids have overdosed from your pills. That's three funerals and three families mourning because of you. How does that make you feel?

AARON

I don't give a fuck about them or you, you lit...

MAGGIE interrupts AARON with a hard punch to his face.

MAGGIE

(YELLS)

FIFTY-ONE!

CUT TO:

OPENING CREDIT SEQUENCE.

WE WATCH MAGGIE in a MONTAGE at the DEA TRAINING ACADEMY with the opening credits.

"*MAGGIE MAY*" performed by "*ROD STEWART*" plays over the opening credits.

MONTAGE.

We see Maggie run laps with other cadets. She leads the pack.

We now see Maggie maneuver through an obstacle course. She passes by an Instructor who clicks a stop watch. The instructor looks impressed.

We now see Maggie at a desk. Other cadets as well. She is engrossed in an exam. She works fast with her number two pencil.

We now see Maggie in a classroom environment. An Instructor teaches from a blackboard. Maggie has her books open and takes notes.

We now see Maggie in a gym setting learning martial arts. She spares against a bigger male opponent. She takes him down despite the size difference.

We now see Maggie at a firing range. She fires her weapon and hits her target exceptionally.

We now see Maggie in full uniform on graduation day. She smiles proudly.

END MONTAGE.

FADE OUT:

FADE BACK IN:

INT. AIRPLANE -- MOVING -- EVENING

MAGGIE sits quietly in her window seat.

MAGGIE (V.O.)
Kate went on to testify later that month.With my evidence and her testimony we went on to put that prick Aaron away for life. I hope he rots away slowly. That concluded my work in Miami.
(beat)
It wasn't long after the Aaron case that I got the call. They needed me in New York. Something very big was going on in New York City and they needed a female agent. That agent was me.
(beat)
But I needed to go home first. So they gave me a couple of days' leave to get my head straight and to see my family.
(beat)
I wanted to visit my brother.

A slow day for the Airlines. Only about a DOZEN or so people on this evening's flight. A lone FLIGHT ATTENDANT walks the aisles. A sure easy flight for her.

Didn't make a difference to MAGGIE. She needed some rest and the less people on the plane the better. There was one COUPLE that did manage to peak her curiosity.

POV MAGGIE:

Looks over across the seats and notices two guys sitting next to each other holding hands.

She smiles with comfort and leans back into the cushion of her seat. She nestles her head soothingly and closes her eyes.

FADE TO BLACK:

FADE BACK IN:

INT. ICE SKATING RINK -- EVENING

SUPERIMPOSE ON SCREEN: DOWNTOWN CHICAGO 1990

ANGLE ON:

A 10-YEAR-OLD MAGGIE MAY O'BRIAN.

She looks the same, just with more freckles. She wears tights and a skating dress with leg warmers pulled up over them.

She skates around the ICE RINK with ease. Her footing is good and her form is strong and determined.

The Rink is of a modest size with a few hundred Bleacher Seats circled around it. SCRAPES and SCRATCHES can be seen on the ice itself from various other ice skaters or hockey players from that day.

MAGGIE stops in her skating routine to the sound of clapping.
P.O.V. MAGGIE:

She sees her older brother SEAN in the empty bleachers. He claps for his baby sister with a standing ovation.

SEAN is 17, tall and skinny with black hair and blue eyes. He wears a trendy outfit.

MAGGIE startles a bit but then realizes it's SEAN.

MAGGIE

You scared me.

(beat)

How long have you been watching me?

SEAN

Long enough to see how talented you are. Maggie May O'Brian . . .

(opens his arms)

. . . the next Olympic gold medalist.

MAGGIE

Yeah, right!

(smiles)

Well, maybe silver.

SEAN laughs and walks down the bleacher steps.

SEAN

Come on. Dad let me leave the bar early to walk you home. He wasn't looking too good if you can catch my drift.

SEAN pretends to stumble like a drunk person. The TWO laugh with each other.

In walks COACH LYNCH, MAGGIE's ice skating instructor. He is a very well-conditioned athlete. Six foot two, a hundred and eighty five pounds. He has blond hair and blue eyes.

COACH LYNCH

I thought I heard voices.

(looks at Maggie)

I thought I told you only another ten minutes.

MAGGIE

I know, Coach, but I wanted to keep practicing.

SEAN

Hey, Coach Lynch, you know you have yourself a little gold medalist here.

COACH LYNCH

She definitely has the heart of a champion.

MAGGIE blushes.

COACH LYNCH

Come on, you two, it's getting late.

(playfully)

Your father would kill me if he knew you were still here.

(smiles)

Especially if I started charging him for ice time.

SEAN

Don't worry 'bout that, Coach Lynch. You can drink off her ice time at the pub.

COACH LYNCH
(laughs)
Very funny, Sean.
(beat)
Come on...you two get out of here. I need to lock up.

SEAN
You got it. Come on Maggs.

DISSOLVE TO:

EXT. STREET -- MOVING - EVENING

WE MOVE over the VOICE OVER as MAGGIE and SEAN exit the Ice Rink.

MAGGIE (V.O.)
He was the only one who ever called me Maggs. I didn't mind. I thought it was cool. I thought he was the coolest.
(beat)
Coach Lynch let me skate for free, cause my father could barely afford to keep a roof over our heads, let alone pay for my lessons. I mean we weren't poor, but there were five of us. My father owned a local pub in town where he and my mom worked.
(beat)
Sean bar-backed for tips most of the time and my sister Tricia would waitress on the weekends. My oldest sister, Michelle, moved to Texas to work as a flight attendant. She always wanted to travel. And my other brother Brian didn't do much but get into trouble.

MAGGIE and SEAN stroll down the street. MAGGIE reaches up to hold SEAN's hand.

MAGGIE (V.O.)
The rink wasn't too far from our house. And I loved it when Sean would come to get me. My father most of the time would be drunk. My mom, too.
(beat)
I remember that night like it was yesterday. That name Tommy Macallister will always be with me.

SEAN holds up a piece of METAL FENCE for MAGGIE to scoot under. An apparent short cut found by SEAN.

SEAN
Come on, Maggs.

MAGGIE ducks underneath and follows SEAN. They cross through a small field and exit back out onto the street.

SEAN (CONT'D)
So, when is your next practice?

MAGGIE
Thursday. You going come get me?

SEAN
(smiles)
Of course I will.

SEAN sees headlights approach. He puts up his hand to shade the light from his eyes.

A black NISSAN SENTRA moves into VIEW.

ANGLE ON:

MIKE MAHONEY

He is 17, tall and thin with black hair and brown eyes. He's a gentle guy and very soft spoken.

MIKE
Hey, Sean.

SEAN recognizes him.

SEAN
Hey, Mike. What's up?

MIKE
Can I talk to you for a minute?
(looks at Maggie)
Hey, Maggie.

MAGGIE likes MIKE.

MAGGIE
Hi, Mike.

SEAN
(to Maggie)
Give me a minute. I'll be right back.

MAGGIE nods her head and walks over to the curb and takes a seat. SEAN walks over to the car and leans into the window.

MIKE
Where have you been?
(beat)
I haven't heard from you in almost a week. I only live three houses down and you act like we live in different states.

SEAN
I know, I know. I'm sorry. But you know how my father is.
(beat)
This is very difficult for me.

MIKE
I called you like a hundred times and you haven't been to school in two days.
(beat)
Are you avoiding me?

SEAN
No. No not at all. I've been sick, that's all.

MIKE
Are you telling me the truth?
(beat)
'Cause I've heard things.

SEAN
What things?

MIKE
You promise you won't get mad?

SEAN
Promise!
(beat)
What things?

MIKE
I heard you've been hanging out with Tommy Macallister.
(beat)
Is that true? Are you two...

SEAN cuts him off.

SEAN
No. No, well . . .
(stutters)
Yeah . . . the other day. But it was nothing.

MIKE
You know I thought you and I had something.

SEAN
It's not like that. He's just a friend.

MIKE
It's not that other thing I hope.

SEAN
What other thing? What are you talking about?

MIKE reaches over quickly and pulls up SEAN's right sleeve on his shirt.

CLOSE UP:

There are NEEDLE MARKS along SEAN's right arm.

SEAN quickly pulls his arm away and rolls his sleeve back down.

SEAN (CONT'D)
(nervously)
What are you doing?

MIKE
That's what I was afraid off. So, it is true.
(angers)
That shit can kill you. Don't you understand that?

SEAN peers over his shoulder to make sure MAGGIE didn't hear MIKE.

SEAN
I only tried it a couple of times. No big deal.

MIKE
(angers even more)
A COUPLE OF TIMES!

SEAN gets really nervous.

SEAN
SHHH! Are you trying to get me caught? It's no big Deal, I said.

MIKE puts his hand on top of SEAN's hand.

MIKE
I don't want anything to happen to you. I care about you. Tommy is a drug dealer who worry's only about money. Not the people he could hurt.

SEAN smiles and embraces MIKE's hand back.

SEAN
Don't worry. It's just for fun. Sometimes I need to escape.

It now becomes apparent to us that MIKE and SEAN are gay.

MIKE
Do you guys need a ride?

SEAN
Naaa, let us finish our walk. We're almost home.

MIKE
Can I see you tomorrow?

SEAN
(smiles)
Sure.

SEAN glances over towards MAGGIE to make sure she wasn't paying attention. With a moment to himself, SEAN leans into the car and gives MIKE a quick peck on his lips.

SEAN (CONT'D)
I'll see you tomorrow!

MIKE's and SEAN's hands embrace. As MIKE pulls away, their hands slowly slide off of one another.

DISSOLVE TO:

EXT. MAGGIE'S HOUSE - LATER THAT NIGHT

MAGGIE and SEAN saunter up a concrete walkway. A few hedges run parallel with the walkway. Up in front of them is their house.

A white, high ranch with four bedrooms and two bathrooms. The house is upper-middle class with a five-step porch leading to the doorway.

MAGGIE blurts out a peculiar question to SEAN.

MAGGIE
Who's Tommy Macallister?

SEAN's face wrinkles with worry at her question.

SEAN
Were you listening to me and Mike?

MAGGIE
No, but I did hear Mike say that name. Who is he?

SEAN
Nobody important. Just a friend from school.

The TWO enter the house.

INT. MAGGIE'S HOUSE - CONTINUOUS

The inside of the house is decorated in a Retro-Eighties style decor. Lots of bright-colored rugs with matching wallpaper. The couches are covered with plastic slips and a new 32" Zenith television sits proudly in the living room.

About six or seven feet from the front door entrance is a staircase that leads to the second floor. And waiting at the top of that staircase is TRICIA.

TRICIA is 18, slim, with blond hair and blue eyes. She wasn't that tall but tall enough not to be considered short.

TRICIA
(annoyed)
Well, it's about time the two of you got home.
(folds her arms)
Come on, Maggie. Mom wants me to give you a bath and help you with your homework.

MAGGIE
(proudly)
I did my homework already.

TRICIA
(smiles)
Good girl. Then come on . . . . I'll run you a bath and check it over.
(to Sean)
Dad called. He wants you to go back to the bar and help clean up.

MAGGIE starts to walk towards TRICIA.

SEAN
(frowns)
Great!
(beat)
Where's mom?

TRICIA
She's upstairs lying down. She just got home a little while ago.
(beat)
I think her and dad are fighting again.

IN WALKS BRIAN the second youngest. He wears a "*GUNS and ROSES*" t-shirt. He's 13, with long rebellious brown hair and a bad attitude. He's short and stocky with brown eyes.

BRIAN
What else is new! All they do is fight and drink. Drink and fight.
(beat)
Surprised they had time enough to make us.

SEAN
Hey, have a little respect. They are still our parents no matter what.

BRIAN

Whatever!

(beat)

Anyway, a guy named Tommy Macallister came by while you were gone. He told me to tell you to get in touch with him as soon as possible. He has something for you.

SEAN throws a look to MAGGIE, who looks down at him from the staircase.

SEAN

Really?

BRIAN

Yeah, really. Mike from down the block called about ten times, too. Do you owe him money or something?

SEAN

I already saw him and that's none of your business.

BRIAN

(rolls his eyes)

Whatever!

TRICIA

Oh, before I forget, Michelle called long distance from Texas earlier. She would like to hear from the two of you whenever you get the chance.

BRIAN

Is she flying jets yet or what?

TRICIA

She's training to be a stewardess, you terd, not a pilot. Call her. She misses you two.

SEAN

I'll call her tomorrow.

TRICIA thinks a minute. She embraces MAGGIE's hand at the top of the staircase.

TRICIA

(to Sean)

That name Tommy Macallister. I heard that name before. Who is he again?

SEAN
He plays football for Calhoun High.

TRICIA
The Calhoun Cougars. Our rivals.

SEAN
Relax, he's just a friend.

BRIAN
(chuckles)
His boyfriend.

SEAN
(angers)
Shut your mouth . . . loser!

BRIAN
Yeah, I'm the loser. I hear what people say about you.

SEAN
SHUT UP! SHUT UP!

SEAN loses his temper and goes after BRAIN. He forcefully pushes him against a nearby wall. BRIAN stumbles backwards and hits the wall rather hard.

ANGLE ON:

A PICTURE of the entire O'BRIAN FAMILY smashes on the floor.

TRICIA
(yells)
STOP IT! STOP IT!

BRIAN pushes SEAN back and grabs him around the waist. MAGGIE rushes down the staircase and tries to pull BRIAN off of SEAN. She is thrown to the floor.

MAGGIE begins to sob. TRICIA runs down the staircase to help MAGGIE.

SEAN and BRIAN now wrestle each other on the ground trying to outmatch each other's strength.

BRIAN
(while wrestling)
I'm a loser. At least I like girls.

SEAN
(while wrestling)
Yeah. What girls like you?

TRICIA
You two stop it! Stop it now!

TRICIA tries to get between the TWO and she is thrown to the floor onto her elbow.

Suddenly a WOMAN's VOICE is heard from the top of the staircase.

WOMAN'S VOICE (O.S.)
(yells)
KNOCK IT OFF! KNOCK IT OFF NOW!

ALL look up at the top of the staircase.

There stands MAUREEN O'BRIAN, their mother. She looks a little disheveled with her shirt undone from her skirt. She's in her early 40's, thin, about five-six with medium-length auburn hair and brown eyes.

MAUREEN
Sean, get down to the bar now and help your father.
He'll be closing up soon.

SEAN pulls himself away from BRIAN aggressively.

SEAN
(angry)
I HATE IT HERE. I CAN'T WAIT TO LEAVE!

SEAN opens the door and slams it shut.

MAUREEN
Tricia, take your sister upstairs and run her a bath.

TRICIA holds her elbow as she shoves her way past BRIAN. She helps the sniffling MAGGIE to her feet.

TRICIA
(softly to Maggie)
You all right?

MAGGIE nods with tears in her eyes. The TWO move up the staircase past MAUREEN.

MAUREEN
(to Brian)
And you . . .
(points to the glass)
. . . clean that up. I don't want to see a single piece of glass left on that floor.

BRIAN stands there, motionless and out of breath.

MAUREEN (CONT'D)
(raises her eyebrows)
NOW!

BRIAN
Fine! I'll clean it!

BRIAN storms off to get a broom. MAUREEN turns to head back to her bedroom.

DISSOLVE TO:

INT. KEYSTONE PUB AND GRILL - LATER

The bar is a decent size and is decorated in an IRISH DECOR. A few pool tables hide in the back room and a dozen or so dinner tables line themselves along the left side of the front room.

Some of the LOCAL drinkers mill about inside the bar, engrossed in their own conversations.

Behind the bar itself is JACK O'BRIAN. He's six-three, two hundred pounds. His black hair is noticeably thinning and his waist is in the midst of creating a forceful beer-belly.

He pours a draft beer from one of the nearby spouts. He levels off the foam and heads down to his right towards a thirsty customer.

WE RECOGNIZE COACH LYNCH.

JACK
Here you go, Coach.
(slides it to him)
Nice and cold.

COACH LYNCH takes the beer and sips it satisfyingly. He licks his lips to remove the beer froth.

COACH LYNCH
I told you, Jack, call me Billy.

JACK smiles.

JACK
No problem, William.

BILLY reaches into his pocket and slides JACK a ten dollar bill. JACK in return slides the ten dollar bill back to him.

JACK (CONT'D)
Don't insult me, Billy. You take care of my kid, I take care of you.

The TWO smile at each other appreciatively.

BILLY
A little slow in here tonight, huh?

JACK
Ehh, it comes and goes. It slowed down a little while ago so Maureen went home.

JACK cracks himself open a bottled beer from the ice chest and then pull out TWO shot glasses. He slams one down in front of BILLY. He reaches behind him and removes a bottle of JACK DANIEL'S from the tier of numerous bottles behind him.

JACK pours the TWO shots.

BILLY
Whoa . . . easy, Jack. I only came down for a beer or two and maybe one of your famous burgers.

JACK
(seriously)
You gonna insult me twice in the same night?
(beat)
Come on, an Irishmen never drinks alone.

JACK raises the shot glass. We can tell he is already drunk.

JACK (CONT'D)
(laughs)
This will curve your appetite!

BILLY smiles and reluctantly raises the glass. The TWO throw back the harsh shot.

BILLY's face wrinkles. JACK doesn't even flinch from the shot. He then tosses back a beer like it was a glass of cold spring water. He throws the empty into a bin and reaches for another one.

BILLY
(concerned)
You should slow down, Jack.

JACK
Slow down?
(slurs)
I'm just getting started.

IN WALKS SEAN.

He's all distressed from his recent fallout with BRIAN. JACK picks up on his body language. He thinks SEAN's annoyed at the fact that he has to work. He reaches over and grabs for the bottle of JACK DANIEL'S.

He pours himself a shot.

JACK (CONT'D)
(sarcastically)
Ohh . . . is pretty boy upset he has to work?

JACK slugs back the shot. This time he keeps the bottle right in front of him.

SEAN walks by JACK with a sneer and a comment of his own.

SEAN
(under his breath)
Is that your first or second bottle?

JACK infuriates.

JACK
What did you say to me, boy?

SEAN plays it off and notices BILLY.

SEAN
Hey, Coach, long time no see.
(smiles)
Collecting on that ice time?

BILLY
Hey, Sean.
(laughs)
I guess so.

JACK pours another shot and slugs it back.

JACK
(to Billy)
There's my oldest boy. Maybe he should join the ice skating team. I'm sure he would love to wear a pair of tights.

SEAN stops in his tracks. His temper now begins to swell. JACK takes notice.

JACK (CONT'D)
What, boy? You have something to say?

BILLY
(calmly)
Hey, Jack. Take it easy.

JACK
(angers)
Don't tell me how to talk to my kid!

JACK walks from around the bar towards the SEAN, still shocked and as frozen as a statue. The bottle palmed in his grasp.

JACK (CONT'D)
What, boy? You're telling me that you wouldn't love to prance around in a pair of tights?
(laughs smugly)
You could be the center of attention, and I would be so proud.

JACK puts the bottle to his lips.

CLOSE UP:

WE WATCH the bottle touch his lips as he sips.

JACK (CONT'D)
I know all about your little boyfriend Mike down the block. Did you think I would never find out?

BILLY
Hey, Jack, that's enough!

JACK
(angry)
STAY CLEAR OF MY BUSINESS, BILL!
(beat)
This is between a father and his son. Or should I say, daughter.

BILLY
Jack, you had too much to drink. Please.

SEAN trembles with frustration. The CUSTOMERS inside the bar are now locked into this fight. ONE CUSTOMER gets up and leaves.

JACK continues his drunken rage.

JACK
That's right, boy. Get mad!
(beat)
Show me some balls for once in your life.

SEAN spins around with total frustration. Tears stream down his eyes.

SEAN
Show some balls, dad! Is that what you want? I'll tell you what takes balls.
(beat)
How about living in a house where you are the

constant outcast. Always looked at like you're diseased.

(beat)

Or how about not being loved by your own father. How's that for balls? Or how about never getting love from a mother who I hardly ever get to see because she's so god damn loaded all the time. How—

JACK slaps SEAN right across his face.

JACK

Don't you ever talk about your mother like that again.

BILLY rushes JACK and wraps his arms around him.

BILLY

JACK! THAT'S ENOUGH!

JACK struggles a bit, but BILLY is strong.

JACK

THAT'S ENOUGH? I'll tell you when it's enough.

(struggles)

Let me go!

SEAN cries horribly. His face is now beet red.

SEAN

You know what's sad, dad? That's the most you have touched me in years.

(wipes the tears from his eyes)

Not a handshake, not a hug, or even a pat on the back.

(angrily)

I GET A FUCKIN' SLAP BECAUSE I'M DIFFERENT!

SEAN swats the bottle of JACK DANIEL'S from JACK'S hand. The bottle crashes to the floor.

SEAN (CONT'D)

That's your son now.

(beat)

Jack and his son Jack. How fitting.

SEAN runs out of the door and out of the bar.

BILLY
SEAN! SEAN!

BILLY lets JACK out of his grasp.

BILLY (CONT'D)
What is wrong with you?

JACK turns away from BILLY and walks back behind the bar.

JACK
Not me.
(takes a breath)
What's wrong with my son?

FADE TO BLACK:

MAGGIE (V.O.)
I don't know what exactly was said that night. Only those who were there know. All I remember was Sean promised to pick me up that next Thursday night. He forgot. Sean never forgot to pick me up.

FADE IN:

EXT. STREET -- MOVING - NIGHT

MAGGIE ambles down a dark street carrying her skating bag. She peers every minute or so behind her, hoping SEAN would show. He never does.

She makes it within a block of her house when she notices something in the distance.

P.O.V. MAGGIE:

She sees BLUE and RED flashing lights in front of her house. She begins to walk faster and faster.

Suddenly a car approaches from behind.

WE HEAR a horn "*HONK.*"

The car pulls up. A black CHEVY CAMERO.

SEAN (O.S.)
MAGGS! MAGGS!

SEAN sticks his head out of the passenger seat window.

HE opens the door and stumbles out. He is apparently high on something. He giggles uncontrollably and his eyes are glazed over.

MAGGIE glances into the car.

CLOSE UP:

The man in the car hands SEAN a SMALL PACKAGE. SEAN quickly slides it into his back pocket.

SEAN (CONT'D)
Thanks, Tommy.

WE MOVE IN SLOW MOTION.

MAGGIE looks into the car at the driver that WE NOW RECOGNIZE as the infamous TOMMY MACALLISTER. He wears a FOOTBALL JERSEY with the number **52** on it. His eyes a piercing blue and his hair spiked like a porcupine.

The TWO lock eyes for what seems like an eternity. The door slams shut and MAGGIE breaks her eye contact.

TOMMY MACALLISTER drives away like a ghost in the night.

SEAN (CONT'D)
Maggs, I'm sorry. I was running late and I lost track of time. I had to go somewhere with Tommy.

MAGGIE eyes up SEAN.

MAGGIE
Are you okay?

SEAN
Yeah, fine.
(beat)
Never better.

SEAN finally notices the flashing lights in front of his house. He sobers up rather quickly.

SEAN (CONT'D)
(nervously)
What happened?
(takes Maggie's hand)
Come on.

The TWO hurry down the street.

EXT. MAGGIE'S HOUSE - MOMENTS LATER

There are three PATROL CARS in front of their house. FOUR CHICAGO POLICE OFFICERS stand outside.

MAGGIE and SEAN enter FRAME.

P.O.V. SEAN:

As SEAN passes one of the Patrol Cars, he sees JACK in the back seat. His hands handcuffed behind his back.

JACK looks up at SEAN and then looks away and hangs his head in shame.

An OFFICER recognizes SEAN and MAGGIE.

OFFICER
Sean.

SEAN nervously approaches the OFFICER, who waves the TWO over from the front lawn.

The other OFFICERS mill about.

SEAN
Officer Milestone. What happened?

MAGGIE stands next to SEAN. She handles all the commotion well. Her body language shows us that she is used to it.

OFFICER MILESTONE tries to remember MAGGIE's name.

OFFICER MILESTONE
Hi there, Meghan. How's the little ballerina today?

MAGGIE wrinkles her face.

MAGGIE
My name is Maggie
(beat)
And I'm not a ballerina. I'm going to be a famous ice skater one day.

SEAN smiles and brushes her hair back from her innocent face.

SEAN
That's right, Maggs . . .and don't let anyone ever tell you what or who to be. Always be yourself.

OFFICER MILESTONE is a little embarrassed from his mistake.

OFFICER MILESTONE
(to Sean)
Sorry.

SEAN
So what's going on?

OFFICER MILESTONE
We're taking your father in for the night. Apparently he had a few too many and him and your mom had a pretty bad argument that got ugly. A neighbor called it in. Said they heard a lot of screaming and glass breaking.

SEAN
Is my mom all right?

OFFICER MILESTONE
Your mom is fine. She's upstairs with your sister Tricia. Your mother wasn't exactly sober either. I'm sure they will work it out tomorrow. Not to worry. We'll take your father in and let him sleep it off.

BRIAN walks into FRAME out from some bushes. He wears an "*IRON MAIDEN*" t-shirt.

BRIAN
Yeah, let him sleep it off.

"ALL" turn to BRIAN.

OFFICER MILESTONE
Where did you come from?

BRIAN
(slurs)
Why? Is it against the law to take a walk through the woods when your drunken father goes ape shit in the house.

SEAN
Hey, Brian, watch your mouth. He is here to help.

OFFICER MILESTONE understands BRIAN's pain. He doesn't make a big deal out of his little outburst.

BRIAN
Whatever!
(slurs)
We are just one big happy family.

SEAN maintains his composure. OFFICER MILESTONE takes notice of BRIAN slurred speech.

OFFICER MILESTONE
Are you all right, Brian? Have you been drinking?

BRIAN chuckles a bit.

BRIAN
It's all in the family.

SEAN plays it off.

SEAN
I'll take care of him, Officer Milestone. No problems here.

SEAN pushes BRIAN towards their house.

OFFICER MILESTONE
(reluctantly)
Okay then. Don't worry about your dad. He'll be home tomorrow.
(looks at Brian)
Make sure he gets some rest.

SEAN
Yes, sir, Officer Milestone. I will do that. Right to bed.

OFFICER MILESTONE walks (O.S.). SEAN looks over at BRIAN angrily.

SEAN (CONT'D)
Do you always have to be a dick?

BRIAN
Whatever. And where have you been? You missed all the fun.

SEAN looks down at MAGGIE.

SEAN
I had to get Maggs from skating practice.

MAGGIE keeps up with SEAN's story with a smile.

MAGGIE
Yeah. From practice.

SEAN
And where have you been? Drinking in the woods I suppose.

BRIAN walks past SEAN with an irritating "*BELCH*."

BRIAN
Yeah, so! They do. I will!

BRIAN continues to walk towards the house.

WE SEE the PATROL CARS drive away.

SEAN
Come on, Maggs. Let's go see how mom’s doing.

MAGGIE
Okay.

DISSOLVE TO:

INT. MAGGIE'S HOUSE -- MAGGIE'S ROOM -- LATE NIGHT

MAGGIE MOVEs over the VOICE OVER.

She gets out of bed and walks out of her room into the Hallway.

MAGGIE (V.O.)
That was one of the longest days of my life. I still don't know what woke me up that night, but I wish it never did. What I witnessed that night will be with me until the day I die.

INT. HALLWAY -- MOVING - CONTINUOUS

MAGGIE moves through the Hallway with sleep still in her eyes. She rubs them innocently, trying to gain her focus.

As she makes her way down the Hallway, she notices SEAN's light on and his door half open. She saunters up to the door and peeks through the opening.

P.O.V. MAGGIE:

SEAN sits on his bed with his shirt off. A belt is tied tightly around his right arm. He moves to the left of his bed and picks up a needle. He squirts out some of the liquid inside till it is right. Then he jabs himself with the needle into the vein of his arm and injects Heroin.

MAGGIE is mortified. She stumbles away from the door in utter shock.

A moment of terror passes through MAGGIE's little body. Then suddenly a tremendous "*THUD*" is heard.

MAGGIE rushes to the door and pushes it open. The door flings open with authority and smashes against the wall.

P.O.V. MAGGIE:

SEAN shakes on the floor. The needle is still in his arm. His eyes roll into the back of his head. Spit and drool foam up out of his mouth.

MAGGIE
SEAN! SEAN!

MAGGIE kneels down next to him. She shakes him repeatedly.

MAGGIE (CONT'D)
(hysterically)
WAKE UP, SEAN! WAKE UP!

FADE TO BLACK:

OVER THE FADE TO BLACK WE HEAR MAGGIE.

MAGGIE (O.S.) (CONT'D)
SEAN! SEAN! PLEASE . . . WAKE UP!

FADE IN:

EXT. CEMETERY - MORNING

MAGGIE stands next to a lowered CASKET with flowers on top of it. She stares at the CASKET with tears in her eyes.

MATCH DISSOLVE TO:

EXT. CEMETERY - MORNING

The CASKET turns to grass and now REVEALS SEAN's HEADSTONE.

CAMERA PULLS out to REVEAL present-day MAGGIE.

She stands by the HEADSTONE with tears in her eyes. She holds a single rose in her hand. She kneels down and places the rose on the grave.

MALE VOICE (O.S.)
Maggie May O'Brian. It's been a long time.

MAGGIE stands up and turns around to recognize an older MICHAEL MAHONEY. He holds flowers in his hand.

MAGGIE
Oh my god! Mike. How are you?

The TWO embrace in a hug and a kiss.

MIKE
I'm doing well.

MAGGIE
What have you been doing with yourself?

MIKE
I got into real estate and interior decorating. I'm currently living with my life partner in Florida.
(smiles)
Go figure.

MAGGIE smiles.

MAGGIE
I'm very happy for you.

MIKE
And you? Married? Kids?

MAGGIE
No, not yet.

MIKE
So, the last I heard about you was you went onto college and majored in psychology.

MAGGIE
(smiles)
You heard correctly.

MIKE
And what now?

MAGGIE
I joined the police academy right out of college. Graduated a few years ago.

MIKE
Really? Sounds exciting. So what do you do?

MAGGIE
I work undercover, mostly.

MIKE
Undercover . . . wow. For who?

MAGGIE
Sorry, Mike, I can't really disclose that to you.

MIKE
(smiles)
Mysterious and beautiful. What a combination. Sean would have been proud.

The TWO look down at the HEADSTONE.

MAGGIE
I can't believe how long it has been.

MAGGIE chokes up a bit.

MAGGIE (CONT'D)
I miss him so much.

MIKE
So do I, Maggie. So do I.

MAGGIE
Any word on *you*-know-who?

MIKE
Nope. Last I heard was he moved away after the trial.

MAGGIE closes her eyes and remembers. WE HEAR a GAVEL bang and a JUDGE's VOICE speak over the scene.

MALE JUDGE'S VOICE (O.S.)
NOT GUILTY!

MAGGIE opens her eyes.

MAGGIE
I feel like a drink. You feel like a drink, Mike? I was going to head down to my father's pub. My parents don't know I'm in town yet.

MIKE
Sorry, Maggie. Your father isn't exactly one of my favorite people.

MAGGIE looks at MIKE with understanding.

MIKE (CONT'D)
He never understood Sean, so I don't think he'd Understand me. Even after all this time.

MAGGIE
I understand, Mike. But maybe we can catch up later.
Have dinner or something?

MIKE
I would like that.

MIKE removes a BUSINESS CARD and hands it to MAGGIE.

MIKE (CONT'D)
Don't be a stranger. Call me whenever.
(beat)
I have to leave here. Even after all this time, it is still
hard for me to visit.

MAGGIE
I know, Mike. I know.

MIKE kisses MAGGIE on the cheek. He turns and places the flowers on the grave.

MIKE
(to Sean's headstone)
I miss you Sean. I always will.
(to Maggie)
Talk to you soon?

MAGGIE
Sure.

MIKE turns away and walks off. MAGGIE leans down over SEAN's HEADSTONE and kisses the top of it.

MAGGIE (CONT'D)
He still loves you, Sean. After all this time, he still
loves you.
(beat)
Happy Birthday, Sean. And I will always love you.
Always.

She presses her head gently down on the HEADSTONE.

DISSOLVE TO:

INT. KEYSTONE PUB AND GRILL -- BACK BILLIARD ROOM -- LATER

The song "*WHO DO YOU LOVE*" performed by "GEORGE THOROGOOD" plays in the bar.

ANGLE ON:

A CUE BALL and the TIP of a POOL STICK. The pool stick pulls back and smashes into the cue ball.

WIDE SHOT OF THE POOL TABLE: -- MOMENTS LATER

All the BALLS on the table scatter. The 1 ball and the 5 ball roll into separate pockets.

WE PULL out to REVEAL a stocky, well-built man. He has long brown hair pulled into a ponytail. He wears a black long-sleeved shirt, blue jeans, and boots.

He is an apparent POOL SHARK.

POOL SHARK

SOLIDS!

Standing across from our POOL SHARK are TWO MEN. MAN 1 has BLOND HAIR and MAN 2 has BLACK HAIR. The TWO MEN watch with annoyance.

Our POOL SHARK reaches over and grabs a tall glass of beer from one of the other pool tables not being used. He slugs it back and grabs some CHALK from his pool table. He chalks up his pool stick and begins to call out his shots.

POOL SHARK (CONT'D)

(points with his stick)

Three ball, side pocket.

MAN 1 nods his head.

The POLL SHARK surveys the table and then carefully takes his shot.

ANGLE ON:

The 3 BALL rolls right into the side pocket.

CUT TO:

INT. KEYSTONE PUB AND GRILL -- FRONT -- CONTINUOUS

The bar has been slightly renovated. It is now more up-to-date.

A FEW CUSTOMERS mill about inside. Some are at tables. They eat and drink. THREE CUSTOMERs sit at the bar on stools and drink.

Behind the bar is JACK. His hairline has receded and his beer belly has gotten bigger. He wipes down the bar with a rag.

MAN 1 (O.S.)
(yells)
GOD DAMN IT!

JACK looks toward the Billiard Room. He knows something might happen if the guys keep losing their money. But there is nothing he can do about it.

ENTER MAGGIE.

MAGGIE
Hey, bartender, how about some service over here!

JACK turns around ready to yell. He stops in his tracks when he sees it is MAGGIE.

JACK smiles widely.

JACK
Maggie!

He walks quickly from around the bar. He slings his rag over his shoulder and snatches his youngest daughter in a big bear hug.

JACK (CONT'D)
God, I missed you.

MAGGIE kisses him on the cheek.

MAGGIE
I missed you, too, dad.

JACK
It is good to see you. What a sight for these old man's sore eyes.

MAGGIE taps his belly.

MAGGIE
What do you have in there, twins?

JACK
I don't know, but it does have a mind of its own.

JACK turns around and heads back behind the bar.

JACK (CONT'D)
So what can I get my beautiful daughter to drink?

MAGGIE takes a seat at the bar.

MAGGIE
One of your coldest drafts.

JACK
Coming right up.

JACK pulls out a glass and fills it up.

JACK (CONT'D)
So how's things going?

JACK places the drink in front of her.

JACK (CONT'D)
Haven't seen you in a while. The last I heard was you were in Miami, right.

MAGGIE sips her drink.

MAGGIE
That's right. Just wrapped up a case.

JACK
My youngest daughter. Tough as a bag of rusted bagpipes. I still can't believe you're a cop.
(beat)
So what brings you home?

MAGGIE
I came out to visit Sean, and to tell you and mom I'll be staying in New York City for a while.

JACK
What's in New York?

MAGGIE
My job needs me there for the time being.

JACK
For what?

MAGGIE
Come on, dad, you know I can't tell you that.

JACK
New York City is dangerous, you know. I don't want those sons of—

MAGGIE interrupts.

MAGGIE
Dad, relax. I'll be fine. I don't work alone, you know.

JACK
Well, all I'm saying is I don't want your mother to worry. She has enough on her plate.

MAGGIE
Speaking of mom, where is she?

JACK
Out back, taking a break.

WE HEAR some commotion from the back Billiard Room again.

P.O.V. MAGGIE:

She looks towards the back and sees that the TWO MEN are really upset. MAN 1 hands a wad of cash to our POOL SHARK.

MAN 2 reaches into his back pocket and slams down another wad of CASH on the Pool Table.

MAN 2
AGAIN!

The POOL SHARK glances over at MAGGIE with a glass of beer in his clutches. He slams it back and peers at MAGGIE through the emptiness of the bottom of the glass. He puts the glass down and smiles at MAGGIE.

POOL SHARK
Rack 'em, sweetheart.

MAGGIE laughs.

MAGGIE
I see some things never change.
(beat)
Mom's out back, you said?

JACK
Yeah. Probably smoking.

MAGGIE
Still?

JACK
Yeah, especially today!

MAGGIE
(to Mike)
I'll be right back.
(beat)
I'm going to go talk to mom for a minute.

CUT TO:

EXT. KEYSTONE PUB AND GRILL -- ALLEYWAY -- MOMENTS LATER

MAGGIE's mother, MAUREEN, sits on an old milk crate in front of a garbage dumpster. She puffs on a cigarette with tear tracks in her eyes. She wears a green "*KEYSTONE PUB AND GRILL*" t-shirt tucked into a pair of black jeans.

She has aged relatively well, but her drinking has kept her thin and pale.

MAGGIE exits an Alleyway door and peaks her head outside. She sees MAUREEN.

MAGGIE
Hey there, beautiful. Want some company?

MAUREEN looks over at MAGGIE with a beaming smile. She wipes her eyes and sniffles a little.

MAUREEN
Sure thing, gorgeous. Come on over here and give an old lady a hug.

MAUREEN stands up from the crate, flicks her cigarette, and then stumbles. MAGGIE can tell she has been drinking.

MAGGIE
A little too much, mom?

MAUREEN
It's always too much. Come here and give me that hug.

The TWO embrace in a hug. MAUREEN holds on tight and then kisses her on the cheek.

MAUREEN (CONT'D)
You have been gone awhile.

MAGGIE
Just work.

MAUREEN shakes her head.

MAUREEN
A doctor? A lawyer?
(beat)
You had to be a cop.
(does the sign of the cross)
Jesus, Mary, and Joseph. You kids are going to be the death of me.

MAGGIE
(laughs)
Mom, I'm fine.

MAUREEN
Have you spoken to your sisters?

MAGGIE
Yes. Spoke with Michelle yesterday and Tricia this morning.
(beat)
Tricia's having a ball in Cali. She started at a new gym. She's working hand in hand with another physical therapist. She's doing well.

MAUREEN
You believe Michelle is pregnant again?

MAGGIE
Yeah, she's a little baby maker. So much for her world-traveling plans as a stewardess.

MAUREEN
Flight attendant.

MAGGIE
(smiles)
Right.

MAUREEN
Hey, maybe you can meet a rich husband like her and settle down. Stranger things have happened.

MAGGIE
Not for me, mom. You know that.

MAUREEN
Don't I? Have you spoken with the other one?

MAGGIE
Haven't spoken with him yet, why?

MAUREEN
He's just out of control. He's the complete opposite of you.
(beat)
I stay up at night, praying I never get that phone call. Either he's been arrested or found dead somewhere in a ditch.

MAGGIE
He's gotten that bad?

MAUREEN
Gambling, drinking, I think now drugs. I don't know what to do with him anymore. I really don't.
(beat)
Maybe you can talk with him. Or kick his ass or something.

MAUREEN starts to choke up a bit.

MAUREEN (CONT'D)
He still blames himself, ya know?

MAGGIE
Blame himself for what?

MAUREEN
Sean. He thinks he could of stopped him.

MAUREEN starts to cry again.

MAUREEN (CONT'D)
He loved him. No matter what. I know he did, and so did your father.

MAGGIE embraces her in a tight hug.

MAGGIE
I know, mom. I know they did.
(beat)
Come on inside. Let's get some coffee.

CUT TO:

INT. KEYSTONE PUB AND GRILL -- BACK BILLIARD ROOM - MOMENTS LATER

CLOSE UP:

The 8 BALL drops into a CORNER POCKET.

The POOL SHARK stands there with a huge smile on his face.

POOL SHARK
That will be two hundred big ones, gentlemen.

The TWO MEN are extremely aggravated.

MAN 1
You hustled us, you son of a bitch.

POOL SHARK
Don't hate the player, my friend, hate the game.

MAN 2 moves around to the POOL SHARK'S blind side. MAN 1 looks past the POOL SHARK and knows what's coming.

MAN 1
I want my money back, you cheating asshole.

POOL SHARK
That'll be a cold day in hell.

MAN 2 suddenly smashes an empty GLASS over his head.

MAN 2
Fuck you, asshole.

The POOL SHARK falls forward onto the floor from the surprised blow. His pool stick slips out of his grip and rolls along the floor.

MAN 2 reaches down into his pockets in search of his other winnings. He finds the cash in his front pocket and snatches it like a thief.

He waves the cash in front of the POOL SHARK's eyes.

MAN 2 (CONT'D)
Now we are even, you hustling piece of shit.

CLOSE UP:

WE SEE a black boot step on the pool stick and stop it from rolling.

CAMERA PANS UP to REVEAL MAGGIE.

MAGGIE
Is there a problem here, gentlemen?

MAN 1
Fuck off, lady. This doesn't concern you.

The POOL SHARK starts to regain his composure. He looks up at MAGGIE with a smile. His head bleeds from the hard blow.

POOL SHARK
Hello there, little sister. It's been awhile.
(beat)
You look good.

MAGGIE

Hello, Brian. On all fours, I see. You've definitely have looked better.

BRIAN eyes up MAN 1. He stares right at his groin and quickly balls up his fist and punches MAN 1 in his groin. MAN 1 tumbles down to the ground.

MAN 2 grabs for a pool stick. He reels back to hit BRIAN with it, but MAGGIE steps in. She catches the pool stick in mid-flight and snatches it away from MAN 2. She tosses it to the ground.

MAGGIE (CONT'D)

Now, take it easy.

MAN 2

I never hit a women before, but for you I'll make an exception.

MAGGIE

Come on and try.

MAN 2 swings wildly at MAGGIE. She blocks it easily and then strikes him in his stomach. She hit him so hard in the stomach that as he stumbles backwards he actually throws up at the same time.

MAGGIE (CONT'D)

That's just nasty!

MAN 2

You bitch!

MAN 2 wipes the puke from his face and heads after MAGGIE. He swings at her again. MAGGIE steps to the side with a martial arts side kick to his stomach followed by an elbow thrust to the back of his head.

The momentum of the blow sends MAN 2 into the edge of one of the pool tables. He is knocked unconscious.

MAN 1 comes up from behind MAGGIE and bear-hugs her from the back.

MAN 1

Gotcha!

MAGGIE tries to free her arms but can't. MAN 1 is strong. She holds steady for a bit and then smashes the back of her head into his nose. Blood squirts out from MAN 1's nose as he releases her from his grip.

MAN 1 (CONT'D)
My nose. You bitch. You broke my nose!

MAN 1 angers. He reaches into his back pocket and pulls out a SWITCHBLADE.

MAN 1 (CONT'D)
I'm gonna gut you like a fish.

MAGGIE squares up her stance ready to fight. MAN 1 rushes at her widely. Suddenly, a pool stick smashes him right in the face. The blow is so fierce it breaks the pool stick in half.

The impact sends MAN 1 into a mid-air flip over the top of one of the pool tables.

BRIAN stands there with the broken half of the pool stick. Blood leaks down the side of his face.

BRIAN
Welcome home, sis.
(smiles)
Don't I get a kiss?

SMASH CUT TO:

EXT. KEYSTONE PUB AND GRILL - MOMENTS LATER

BRIAN flies out of the front door of the bar. He lands hard on the concrete outside.

MAGGIE follows right behind him.

MAGGIE
(angry)
You better clean up your act or I will fly back from New York and kick your ass again.
(beat)
Now come inside and have a drink with me.

MAGGIE opens the door and walks back inside the bar.

BRIAN sits there on the sidewalk. He wraps his arms around his knees with a cordial smile.

BRIAN
I've missed you, too, sis!

FADE TO BLACK:

WE HEAR the engine roar of an AIRPLANE. A PILOT speaks over an intercom.

PILOT (O.S.)
Ladies and gentlemen, welcome to New York City. The weather is a chilly 51 degrees. I hope you enjoy your stay. On behalf of myself and my crew, I'd like to thank you for flying American Airlines.

FADE IN:

INT. JFK AIRPORT -- TERMINAL -- MOVING -- EVENING

RANDOM PEOPLE maneuver about. Very crowed. Very uncomfortable.

MAGGIE walks rather quickly down the TERMINAL TUNNEL. Her mind races with thoughts.

MAGGIE (V.O.)
For the first time in a long while, I was nervous and apprehensive. A new city, a new boss and a new roommate. Most people acquire these things throughout their years.
(beat)
I had to get mine all in the same day. I also wondered how I got pushed up so fast. I mean New York City isn't exactly the first place they would send a rookie.
(beat)
Sgt. Jacobs will meet you at the terminal for your new assignment.

She looks up and follows the SIGNs to baggage claim. She maneuvers around people. Her eyes are like a sponge, absorbing all the information it can.

MAGGIE (V.O.) (CONT'D)
Fucking great. What does he look like? You think they would tell me that. How's he going find me? Maybe my red hair will throw up a flag.

P.O.V. MAGGIE:

A middle-aged CAUCASIAN WOMAN weaves in and out of PEOPLE. A BABY strapped to her back, she talks on a BLUE TOOTH and pushes a STROLLER with another BABY inside it.

MAGGIE and the WOMAN pass each other. MAGGIE HEARS the WOMAN speak.

CAUCASIAN WOMAN
All right, honey. I'll see you in five minutes.

MAGGIE (V.O.)
Damn, I wonder how my mom did it with five kids.

MAGGIE approaches the baggage claim. She stands there and waits for the CONVEYER BELT to spit out the luggage.

MAGGIE (V.O.) (CONT'D)
Sgt. Jacobs. I'm guessing white.
(beat)
Jacobs, maybe Jewish, black hair.

The baggage starts to come out. PEOPLE hustle for their baggage. MAGGIE waits for her moment and strikes. She grabs one of her bags and places it between her feet.

MAGGIE (V.O.) (CONT'D)
He's going to have that New York attitude, maybe a slight beer gut, if he's anything like my father.

MAGGIE sees her other bag and lunges for it. She leaves her other bag unattended. She grabs her bag from the conveyer belt and turns around to grab her other bag.

Her other bag is missing.

MAGGIE (CONT'D)
What the hell?

She glances to her left. No bag.

MAGGIE (CONT'D)
What? Where did it . . .

She glances to her right. No bag. She spins around in a circle to all the people in her vicinity. No bag.

MAGGIE (CONT'D)
Great! Just great!
(beat)
I'm in New York for one minute and I already have lost half my wardrobe.

A deep, WOMAN's VOICE catches MAGGIE's attention.

WOMAN'S VOICE (O.S.)
Aren't you familiar with that saying?
(beat)
In a New York minute?

MAGGIE turns around.

P.O.V. MAGGIE:

SGT. SERINA JACOBS stands before MAGGIE. She is an AFRICAN AMERICAN WOMAN with short black hair. She wears a woman's blue business suit with white sneakers. She is a tall woman at five eleven, husky, on the manly side.

She holds MAGGIE's bag in her left hand.

SGT. JACOBS
Maggie O'Brian, I presume?

MAGGIE
Um, yes. Do I know you?

SGT. JACOBS
I'm Sgt. Jacobs. Sgt. Serina Jacobs.

MAGGIE eyes her up and down. She can't help but notice her sneakers. SGT. JACOBS looks down at her feet.

SGT. JACOBS (CONT'D)
It's late and my feet hurt. So do my shoulders. Here.

She gives MAGGIE back her bag.

SGT. JACOBS (CONT'D)
I'm not a doorman.

MAGGIE takes back her bag.

SGT. JACOBS (CONT'D)
Let's go, Maggie. We have a lot to go over and little time to do so. And let's keep the questions at a minimal until I get my coffee.
(beat)
Follow me.

SGT. JACOBS takes off. MAGGIE slings her bags over her shoulders and hustles behind her.

MAGGIE (V.O.)
Man, was I way off with that one.

DISSOLVE TO:

INT. CAR -- MOVING - MOMENTS LATER

SGT. JACOBS sips on a big cup of coffee. She weaves in and out of TRAFFIC like a race car driver.

SGT. JACOBS
(sips her coffee)
I read your jacket. Not too bad. Pretty impressive for such a young agent.

MAGGIE
Thanks.

SGT. JACOBS sips her coffee again.

SGT. JACOBS
Let's see if I got this correct. Maggie May O'Brian, born and raised in Chicago. Parents, Maureen and Jack, still alive and still in Chicago. Sisters, Tricia, Michelle one in Texas and one in California. Two brothers, Sean, deceased and Brian who still lives in Chicago.
(beat)
Scored high on all exams and ranked third in her graduating class at the academy. Graduated with a 3.9 gpa and a psychology degree from Cornell University. Not to mention a second degree black belt in Tae Kwon Do. Did I miss anything?

MAGGIE
I also ice skate.

SGT. JACOBS
Won the amateur trophy for girls five years in a row.

MAGGIE smiles.

MAGGIE
Bet you don't know who my first boyfriend was.

SGT. JACOBS
No, I don't. Do you?

They BOTH chuckle and laugh with each other.

MAGGIE
So, tell me something about my new partner? She's a female, that much I know. What's she like?

SGT. JACOBS
Well, she's mostly like you, just a few years older. Highly motivated and tough as nails. She and her partner were so close to catching that son of a bitch G.o.n.y.

MAGGIE
What the hell is a G.o.n.y.?

SGT. JACOBS puts her coffee into a cup holder and reaches for the back seat, her eyes still on the road.

She pulls forward a FOLDER about three inches thick. She tosses it on Maggie's lap.

SGT. JACOBS
G.o.n.y. is your assignment. G.o.n.y. and the three spirits. You better brush up fast. Because if I know Justine, she is going to want to get right to work.

MAGGIE fans through the FOLDER.

MAGGIE
G.o.n.y. and the three spirits? Did I just walk into a horror movie?

SGT. JACOBS
Nope! You just walked into a war and you are my new weapon.

SGT. JACOBS looks over at MAGGIE.

SGT. JACOBS (CONT'D)
Are you ready for it or did I choose the wrong person for the job?

MAGGIE looks back at SGT. JACOBS, convincingly.

MAGGIE
Start from the beginning.

SGT. JACOBS
Good! I hope you're taking notes.
(beat)
G.o.n.y. is one of the worst crime lords New York has had in a long time. He's never been seen, only heard of. We have no surveillance on him and no evidence on him. G.o.n.y. . . .
(beat)
. . . Ghost of New York.

MAGGIE
Ghost of New York?

SGT. JACOBS
That's right. His crew is the three spirits. The Boogeyman, the Sandman, and Candyman. They are the evidence that such a person exists. It is said that's who they work for. We have some stuff on them but nothing solid enough to lead to G.o.n.y. They run coke, heroin, and those fantasy pills the kids like to take.

MAGGIE
Who supplies them?

SGT. JACOBS

That's the kicker. G.o.n.y. uses all the other dealers as his suppliers. He cuts in on their action, taking whatever he wants. Either you cut him in or he cuts you out permanently. He has the Italians and Colombians working for him. The Jamaicans fear him, and he just recently did a full on hit to the Chinese down in Chinatown. A real bloodbath.

FLASHBACK TO:

INT. WAREHOUSE - NIGHT

A tall, thin AFRICAN AMERICAN MAN named SLIM stands in the middle of a dimly-lit warehouse. He wears a nice black suit with shoes to match. His face is well-shaven and his hair is cut short. He's in his early forties and loves himself.

A long, menthol cigarette dangles from his mouth. He stands there agitated in his body language. Every minute or so he peers down at his Rolex watch.

Hundreds of boxes can be seen around him. The boxes have Chinese lettering written on them.

He takes the last drag of his cigarette and drops it to the floor. The cigarette lands next to THREE other cigarettes that have already been smoked. He steps on the fourth and rubs it out with his shoe.

WE HEAR the sound of footsteps in the silence of the warehouse.

FIVE CHINESE MEN emerge out of the darkness and place themselves about fifteen feet away from SLIM. They, too, are well-dressed.

The FIVE MEN stand there in silence.

SLIM

(cockily)

Gentlemen, it is about god damn time! I am a very busy man. Does your boss plan on joining us anytime soon, or what?

The FIVE MEN stand there without comment.

SLIM (CONT'D)
(snaps his fingers)
Do you speak English? I've been waiting for over half an hour. My employer will not be happy.

Another FIGURE emerges from out of the darkness. He is an older CHINESE MAN in his late fifties. Very well dressed and powerful in his demeanor.

His name is CHOW LANG. One of the heads of the CHINESE TRIADS. He walks out and stands behind his men. He holds a BRIEFCASE in his hand.

CHOW (Chinese Accent)
On the contrary, Mr. Slim, they speak perfect English. They just choose not to speak with the likes of you.

SLIM
Oh, now that's cold. But I'm not here to talk. I am here to do business.

CHOW puts down the briefcase.

CHOW (Chinese Accent)
Is that what you call what you do? Business?

SLIM
Yeah. Business.

CHOW (Chinese Accent)
But you are all alone. What kind of man does business like this without men by his side?

SLIM opens his suit jacket and reveals TWO NINE MILLIMETERS in holsters.

SLIM
Don't get it twisted, Chow.
(beat)
I'm real surgical with these bitches.

SLIM closes his jacket.

CHOW (Chinese Accent)
But a man that walks alone is a man that cannot be trusted.

SLIM

Enough of this fortune cookie shit.

SLIM waves his hand around the area.

SLIM (CONT'D)

I'm never alone, Chow.

(beat)

The spirits are always amongst us.

From the rafters of the Warehouse, TWO RED BEAMS shoot out of the darkness. One BEAM from the right side of the warehouse and one BEAM from the left side of the warehouse.

Both BEAMS aim right on CHOW's forehead.

The FIVE CHINESE MEN panic and draw their weapons.

SLIM (CONT'D)

You better tell them to cool out, Chow.

CHOW keeps his composure.

CHOW (Chinese Accent)

Put away your weapons, men.

(beat)

Like Mr. Slim said, we are here to talk business.

The FIVE CHINESE MEN put away their weapons.

SLIM

My employer is tired of your delays. Are you in or out?

CHOW (Chinese Accent)

And what is this so called proposition?

SLIM

Thirty percent of your take of the heroin business.

CHOW angers.

CHOW (Chinese Accent)

You are mad! Mr. Shung will never agree to those terms.

SLIM
Then I guess you don't value your family's lives?
(beat)
Your wife, Lily, and your daughter, Lin.

SLIM reaches into his jacket pocket and removes TWO pictures. One is of an older CHINESE WOMAN and the other is of a LITTLE CHINESE GIRL.

SLIM (CONT'D)
All it takes is one phone call, Chow.

CHOW angers even more. He tosses the briefcase over towards SLIM. The briefcase slides across the floor and stops right at SLIM's feet.

CHOW (Chinese Accent)
That is the extent of our deal, Mr. Slim. You've earned every penny of it.

SLIM kneels down to open the briefcase. He opens it to only see that it is empty.

CHOW laughs.

CHOW (Chinese Accent) (CONT'D)
So where is this supposed ghost of New York now, Mr. Slim?

Suddenly CHOW's body jerks forward. A huge KNIFE pushes up through his chest. CHOW screams in horrific pain.

ANGLE ON:

A BLACK, FACELESS MASK appears over the right shoulder of CHOW. All that is exposed is a little slit hole for a mouth and two slits for the eyes. The voice of G.O.N.Y. is distorted from a small VOICE BOX around his throat.

G.O.N.Y. (Voice Box)
I am right behind you, Chow.

G.O.N.Y. pulls CHOW into the darkness of the warehouse.

GUNFIRE rings out from the rafters. TWO of the CHINESE men fall to the ground, dead. SLIM unleashes his weapons from his kneeling position. He takes out the other THREE CHINESE men with a flurry of gunfire.

SLIM stands to his feet and holsters his weapons.

SLIM
What do we do now? I told you the Triads were going to be tough.

G.O.N.Y. speaks from the shadows.

G.O.N.Y. (Voice Box)
We have to make a statement. An extreme statement.

A moment passes.

WE HEAR the sound of a belt open, then a zipper being unzipped, followed by the sound of pants being pulled down.

WE THEN HEAR the sound of something being cut.

G.O.N.Y. (Voice Box) (CONT'D)
Send this to Shung. It will change his way of thinking.

G.O.N.Y. throws something out from the shadows that lands at SLIM's feet. SLIM's face turns to utter sickness.

SLIM
Jesus Christ! Is that his . . .

G.O.N.Y. interrupts.

G.O.N.Y. (Voice Box)
SEND IT!

CUT TO:

INT. CAR -- MOVING - CONTINUOUS

SGT. JACOBS
Story goes that it was sent to Shung, and well, sources say G.o.n.y. now gets a healthy cut of the heroin business.

MAGGIE
That's one of the worst things I ever heard!

SGT. JACOBS
Well, sweetheart, like I said, you're in the middle of a war.

The car comes to a stop.

SGT. JACOBS (CONT'D)
Are you ready to meet your partner?

MAGGIE
(enthusiastically)
Absolutely!

SMASH CUT TO:

INT. JUSTINE'S APT. - MOMENTS LATER

Hard music plays.

WE SEE hands and feet punch and kick a black HEAVY BAG.

WE PULL out to reveal JUSTINE HANSEN. She is five nine and very attractive. Blond hair with blue eyes and is in incredible shape. She wears workout gear as she practices her martial arts moves on the heavy bag.

She sweats hard. She does a few front kicks and then drops to the floor to do push-ups.

WE WATCH her do numerous push-ups until she starts to weaken. Just when we think she is ready to collapse, she does five more.

She gets up off the floor, grabs a towel from a nearby chair, and wipes her face. She walks over and turns the music off.

At that moment WE HEAR a "*KNOCK*" at her door.

JUSTINE walks over to the door and opens it to see SGT. JACOBS and MAGGIE.

SGT. JACOBS
Justine.

JUSTINE
Sarge, come on in.

SGT. JACOBS and MAGGIE enter the apartment. MAGGIE takes a curios look around.

P.O.V. MAGGIE:

It's a well-furnished, very spacious, two-bedroom apartment. Up to date in its decor. A flat screen t.v. hangs on the wall, nice couches with a small twenty-book library on the left wall. A laptop computer is set up in the kitchen area. Set back deep in the apartment is the heavy bag and some weights.

SGT. JACOBS
Justine this is your new partner, Maggie.
(beat)
Maggie, this is Justine.

MAGGIE extends her hand of friendship. JUSTINE takes a minute to size MAGGIE up.

MAGGIE
Nice to meet—

JUSTINE cuts her off.

JUSTINE
(to Sgt. Jacobs)
So, you think she's up for this?

SGT. JACOBS
She's up for it!

JUSTINE walks away into the Kitchen.

MAGGIE
UMMMM, well, it's nice to meet you, too.

SGT. JACOBS looks at MAGGIE with a grin.

SGT. JACOBS
Don't worry. Give her some time to adjust.

JUSTINE walks back into the room with a bottle of water. She sips on it.

JUSTINE
You got the smaller room in the back.

MAGGIE takes her luggage and tosses it on the floor.

MAGGIE

Why don't I just sleep on the floor. It can't be any colder then this room is!

JUSTINE looks at SGT. JACOBS with a grin.

JUSTINE

Good . . . she has balls.

JUSTINE reaches out her hand to shake MAGGIE's.

JUSTINE (CONT'D)

Nice to meet you. Sorry 'boutthe attitude. Just checking . . . ya know.

MAGGIE

No problem.

SGT. JACOBS

(to Justine)

I got her up to speed. Give her more of the details when she is settled.

SGT. JACOBS raises her eyebrows to JUSTINE.

SGT. JACOBS (CONT'D)

Introduce her to the box. I am sure she is cherry. I have to go. I have a lot to do.

(to Maggie)

Listen to her and learn. She is my best.

MAGGIE nods her head.

SGT. JACOBS (CONT'D)

I'll be in touch. You two take some time to get to know each other.

SGT. JACOBS turns for the door and opens it.

JUSTINE

Later, Sarge.

MAGGIE

Bye.

SGT. JACOBS
Have fun, you two.

She closes the door.

MAGGIE
So now what?

JUSTINE
Make yourself at home. I'm gonna go shower. Why don't you go and unpack, have a drink or give yourself a tour.

MAGGIE smiles. JUSTINE walks off towards the Bathroom and takes off her shirt and exposes her breasts to MAGGIE.

The Bathroom door closes. MAGGIE picks up her suitcases.

MAGGIE
(to herself)
Well, at least I know she's not shy.

MAGGIE walks into the back room, where she is staying.

INT. MAGGIE'S ROOM - CONTINUOUS

The walls are bare white and the queen bed has red Egyptian cotton sheets and two pillows on it already. A large Armoire stands on the left wall and a six-drawer dresser stands on the right wall.

She drops her suitcases on the floor and walks over to the closet. She opens it.

MAGGIE
(to herself)
Not bad, good closet space.

MAGGIE then sits on the bed and kind of bounces on it. She lays back on the soft pillows and closes her eyes for a moment.

FLASHBACK TO:

INT. COURTROOM - MORNING

THE SCENE IS IN A BLURRY BLACK AND WHITE BACKGROUND.

A lone, HISPANIC WOMAN JUROR stands before US.

MALE JUDGE VOICE (O.S.)
Jury, have you reached your verdict?

JUROR
Yes, Judge.
(beat)
We the jury finds Thomas Philip MacAllister not guilty of manslaughter in the first degree.

SUDDENLY MAGGIE'S EYES OPEN.

BACK TO:

INT. MAGGIE'S ROOM - MOMENTS LATER

JUSTINE stands over her.

JUSTINE
Come on . . . get dressed. Something nice and sexy. We're going out!

MAGGIE's still half asleep.

MAGGIE
Umumm . . . okay.

DISSOLVE TO:

INT. JUSTINE'S CAR - LATER

JUSTINE slaps the gears of her brand-new red BMW. She weaves in and out of traffic. MAGGIE and JUSTINE are dressed like foxes.

She slaps the stick shift into third gear and maneuvers around a car.

JUSTINE
So what has the sarge told you?

MAGGIE
She told me about G.o.n.y. and the three spirits. The Ghost of New York. A slippery fish, so I hear.

JUSTINE
That's an understatement.

MAGGIE
What I don't understand is, if you can't find him, how do you know he even exists? Maybe he is just made up.

JUSTINE
Oh, he exists. The one thing is, how do you catch something when you don't know where it is, but it knows everything about you?
(beat)
That's how he stays in business and stays feared.

MAGGIE
It still sounds a little curious.

JUSTINE looks over at MAGGIE.

JUSTINE
Did Sarge tell you anything about my last partner?

MAGGIE
Not very much. She said she would leave that to you.

JUSTINE
His name is John MacDaniels. We call called him "Mac."
(beat)
We were undercover for almost a year, collecting evidence, keeping logs, building our case. And waiting for the day.

MAGGIE
Waiting for what day?

JUSTINE
The day that G.o.n.y. would show his face. And of course he did. When we least expected it.
(beat)
It was late, maybe two or so. Slim had shut down early. We figured he just wanted to party and had some girls paid in full for the night. He called his hotel "The Lion's Den" of New York. It's a cash cow. All rappers and music artists perform and stay in the

hotel. Good business for Slim. Celebrities bring groupies, which means they'll pay anything to stay the night where their favorite artist sleeps. His club is called "The Jungle." It's inside the hotel. That's where we worked . . .

FLASHBACK TO:

INT. THE JUNGLE -- SLIM'S CLUB -- EVENING

The JUNGLE is just like a jungle. Decorated in a jungle atmosphere decor. Plenty of plants both real and fake. Different kind of animal skins cover the bar stools and the V.I.P. chairs and couches. The dance floor and D.J. booth are colored in LEOPARD PRINT. All kinds of animal heads align the walls of the club. Lion heads, gazel heads, rhino heads just to name a few. A small stage can be seen in the back for performers.

The club is closed and the lights are low.

SEVERAL members of a CLEANING CREW mill about and clean.

Behind the main bar is JUSTINE and MAC. MAC is a good-looking man in his mid-thirties. Short blond hair, clean face, tall with a nice build. They both wear WHITE t-shirts that say
"*WELCOME TO THE JUNGLE*."

The TWO wipe down some glasses and the counter.

TWO attractive WOMEN make their way towards MAC. A brunette named CARA and a bleach blond named DEBBIE.

They wear the same t-shirts as MAC and JUSTINE except for the colors. CARA wears a BLUE t-shirt and DEBBIE wears a RED t-shirt.

CARA
We are out of here, Mac.

DEBBIE holds a MONEY POUCH in her hand. It is zipped and locked shut.

DEBBIE
Here is our drawer, Mac.

She hands MAC the POUCH. MAC takes it.

MAC
Are all your receipts and cash accounted for?

DEBBIE

Of course, handsome.

CARA

Hey, Justine. How did you do tonight?

JUSTINE

Pretty good. Still need to count out my drawer.

DEBBIE

(to Justine)

You want us to wait around for you? We're going to paint the town for a little while. Want to come?

JUSTINE

Not tonight. Thanks anyway.

DEBBIE

(to Mac)

What about you, hot stuff? Wanna come out with us?

MAC

(playfully)

You wish.

CARA

(playfully back)

What do we have to do to get you to switch teams?

MAC

(smiles with a wink)

Grow a beard.

They ALL laugh.

DEBBIE

Good night, guys.

MAC

Good night.

CARA

See you later.

JUSTINE

Good night.

DEBBIE and CARA walk (O.S.).

MAC
(to Justine)
If I were straight they wouldn't even talk to me.

JUSTINE
(smiles)
They want what they can't have.

ENTER SLIM. He's dressed sharp as usual. He's a little bit drunk but his instincts are still good. He has THREE HOT GIRLS with him.

SLIM
(to his girls)
Wait by the elevator for me, girls. I'll be right there.

The THREE GIRLS walk towards the elevator and SLIM saunters right up to the bar.

SLIM (CONT'D)
How did your register do tonight, Mac?

MAC
By my count, 'bout six large. I still need to count out my drawer.
(beat)
Here's Debbie and Cara's drawer. They're done for the night. They left already.

MAC hands SLIM the POUCH.

MAC
Feels pretty thick.

SLIM removes a small key from his jacket and opens the POUCH. SLIM reaches inside the POUCH and removes a WAD of cash. He fans through it to inspect it.

SLIM
Not bad. Looks like three, maybe four.
(beat)
But you're still the best bartender I've ever hired, Mac. You keep 'em drinking and coming back.

MAC smiles and nods his head in appreciation.

SLIM
(leans into Mac)
How's the back room?

MAC
Closed up. They all went home as well.

SLIM hands MAC back the POUCH.

SLIM
Do me a favor and go through those receipts. Make sure they're good.

MAC
No problem.

SLIM fans out some of the cash onto the bar.

SLIM
(to Mac)
Here's a little taste for you.
(to Justine)
Come on over here, baby.

JUSTINE smiles and walks down towards SLIM and MAC. SLIM spreads out a couple of hundreds for her and slaps it on the bar.

SLIM (CONT'D)
And a little taste for you.

MAC and JUSTINE take their money and put it into their pockets.

MAC
Thanks, Slim.

JUSTINE
Thanks, Slim.

SLIM opens his jacket and removes a VILE of coke. He dumps a huge pile on the bar. He rolls up a hundred dollar bill and sticks it right into the pile. He inhales deep and takes a good snort.

SLIM pulls his head up.

SLIM

It's going to be a long night for me. I need a little pick me up.

(beat)

You guys in?

MAC shakes his head "*NO*."

MAC

Not tonight, Slim, thanks. If I don't get some sleep I might die.

SLIM

All right, all right, I hear that.

(to Justine)

What about you, Ms. Pretty?

JUSTINE

Why not?

MAC looks at JUSTINE, who looks back at him.

JUSTINE takes the rolled up bill, sticks her nose in the pile, and takes a snort. She tilts her head back and then rubs her nose.

JUSTINE (CONT'D)

Thanks, Slim.

SLIM

I'll leave it. Go ahead and finish it, Gorgeous. That's on Slim.

SLIM slides the VILE back into his pocket.

SLIM (CONT'D)

Mac, before you lock up, I need you to bring me up a couple bottles of Blue Label, some Patrone and some wine for the ladies. Pick something good. I have some friends in Penthouse J.

(beat)

If all goes well tonight, there will be a lot to celebrate.

MAC

No problem, Slim.

SLIM walks off towards an elevator.

SLIM

Ladies. Let's go and meet our guests.

He hits the button and the doors opens. They ALL step inside and the door closes.

MAC takes a wet rag from the bar and quickly wipes away the pile of cocaine off the top. He turns to JUSTINE.

MAC

What were you thinking?

JUSTINE sniffs a little.

JUSTINE

What? I turned him down the last two times. I had no choice.

JUSTINE reaches across the bar and removes a bottle of good wine.

JUSTINE (CONT'D)

Here, this is a good year.

MAC takes it. He then turns around behind him and grabs a bottle of Blue Label.

JUSTINE's a little edgy from the cocaine. MAC takes notice.

MAC

Are you all right?

JUSTINE

I'm fine, come on. Go bring that to Slim so we can get out of here. I'll do the drawer.

MAC

All right.

JUSTINE watches MAC for a second. He looks back at her.

MAC (CONT'D)

What?

JUSTINE

You might get frisked when you go up there, right?

MAC
Shit, you're right.

MAC lifts his right pant leg and unstraps a small Velcro holder with a .38 inside of it. He rolls the loose Velcro around the .38 and hands it to JUSTINE.

MAC (CONT'D)
What would I do without you?

JUSTINE
(smiles)
Blow your cover.

MAC
Very funny.

BACK TO:

INT. JUSTINE'S CAR - CONTINUOUS

MAGGIE
Wait a minute.
(beat)
You actually did coke?

JUSTINE switches gears and passes around a car.

JUSTINE
In this line of work, sometimes doing a line of coke can mean the difference between life or death. Trust is the most important thing you can obtain in this business. If the sharks don't trust you, they will bite you. And let me assure you, they take big bites.

MAGGIE
Fair enough.
(beat)
What happened next?

JUSTINE
This is where everything got out of control . . .

BACK TO:

INT. PENTHOUSE J - LATER

The PENTHOUSE is lavish. Four bedrooms, two bathrooms. Furnished with the top-of-the-line decor.

THREE ITALIAN men stand in front of a desk towards the back of the room. Dressed in Italian suits and very intimidating in their demeanor.

TWO, well dressed, AFRICAN AMERICAN TWINS named LESTER and SIDNEY stand behind the desk. They are big, six-three, two hundred pounds.

The PENTHOUSE ELEVATOR opens.

SLIM exits the elevator with the THREE ESCORTS. They walk towards the others. The ESCORTS take seats on the couch.

SLIM
Gentlemen, gentlemen. Why such serious faces?
(beat)
We are all rich, we have some fine women here and refreshments are on the way.

The ITALIAN MEN gawk at the ESCORTS. The ESCORTS smile back at them.

G.O.N.Y. interrupts SLIM. He enters from another door just right of the desk.

G.O.N.Y. (Voice Box)
There is no time for refreshments.

G.O.N.Y. is in all black attire. From his mask to his gloves. He walks towards the TWINS, crushing the floor with his big black boots. Very broad and tall. At a closer glance we can see a black BULLETPROOF vest fastened around his chest.

SLIM's face drops from the surprise of G.O.N.Y.'s arrival.

SLIM
I didn't know you were here.

G.O.N.Y. (Voice Box)
(threateningly)
I didn't know I had to report to you.

G.O.N.Y. stops right in front of one of the ITALIAN MEN.

G.O.N.Y. (Voice Box) (CONT'D)
Vincent Camellia.

VINCENT (Italian Accent)
This doesn't impress me. Why have you called us here?

G.O.N.Y. (Voice Box)
I have an offer for you.

VINCENT (Italian Accent)
You have an offer for me?
(angrily)
And what might that offer be?

G.O.N.Y. (Voice Box)
I would like to share in the cocaine business with you. Say, about forty percent of it.

VINCENT turns to one of his men and mutters something in Italian.

VINCENT (Italian Accent)
Is that right?

G.O.N.Y. (Voice Box)
That is right. And maybe I won't feed your daughter, Maria, to my pit bulls.

VINCENT looks at G.O.N.Y. in a rage.

At that moment the elevator opens. It is MAC with a pushcart of SLIM's refreshments. He rolls the cart towards everyone.

ALL look towards MAC for a moment, except for VINCENT.

G.O.N.Y. (Voice Box) (CONT'D)
(nervously to Slim)
WHAT THE HELL IS HE DOING HERE?

SLIM
I wanted him to bring some drinks for our guests.

G.O.N.Y. (Voice Box)

You idiot!

VINCENT lunges forward at G.O.N.Y. and grabs his mask.

VINCENT (Italian Accent)

Let me see your face, motherfucker.

VINCENT successfully removes G.O.N.Y.'s mask. He throws the mask into MAC's direction. It lands about three feet in front of him. MAC looks over from his cart and sees G.O.N.Y.'s face. His eyes open wide with disbelief and shock.

G.O.N.Y. quickly ducks away from MAC's view and runs back into the other room.

SLIM fleetly tackles VINCENT over the desk. They roll around and fight.

The TWINS snatch out their weapons and fire at the TWO ITALIAN men. The bullets splatter into their chests. One of them falls backwards onto the ESCORTS.

The ESCORTS scream frantically and run for cover.

MAC reaches down his leg for his .38, when he remembers he left it with JUSTINE.

MAC

Shit.

He looks down at the MASK and grabs it.

The TWINS rush around the desk and subdue VINCENT. They grab him by his arms and slam him down on the desk.

SLIM gets up from behind the desk and glances at MAC. MAC has already made his play for the elevator. He stands inside and pushes the buttons for it to close.

The door starts to close, when suddenly random shots hit MAC through the opening of the closing doors. TWO hit his chest, ONE hits his neck, and ONE hits the right side of his head.

His body jerks backwards into the back part of the elevator. He slams roughly against the elevator wall and slides down into a sitting position.

His blood stains the walls with uneven streaks. G.O.N.Y.'s mask still clutched in his hand.

The elevator door closes.

CUT TO:

INT. THE JUNGLE -- SLIM'S CLUB - MOMENTS LATER

WE HEAR the "*DING*" of the elevator.

JUSTINE
That was fast.

JUSTINE grabs the keys to lock up and looks toward the elevator.

JUSTINE (CONT'D)
Mac.

She gets no answer. She walks around the bar and glances towards the elevator.

JUSTINE (CONT'D)
Mac.

P.O.V. JUSTINE:

She can see MAC full of blood.

JUSTINE yells to the CLEANING CREW.

JUSTINE
CALL AN AMBULANCE, NOW!

ONE of the CLEANING CREW runs off to call the ambulance.

JUSTINE quickly rushes over. She slides to the floor.

JUSTINE (CONT'D)
MAC! MAC!

She immediately checks his pulse. The other TWO members of the CLEANING CREW rush over to help.

CLEANING CREW 1
What happened?

JUSTINE
I don't know. Come on, Mac, speak to me.

CLEANING CREW 2
What's that in his hand?

JUSTINE glances down and sees the MASK in his hand.

JUSTINE
What the hell . . .

She takes the MASK out of MAC's grip. She doesn't realize what she has.

WE THEN HEAR the sound of silenced GUNFIRE. The TWO members of the CLEANING CREW fall to the ground dead.

Before JUSTINE could react, the nozzle of a gun pushes up against her neck just under her ear.

She freezes like a deer in headlights.

G.O.N.Y. (Voice Box)
Don't turn around gorgeous, unless you desire another mouth. Slowly pass that mask back to me.

JUSTINE is scared to death. She carefully reaches back and hands the mask over.

JUSTINE
Please don't kill me. I'm just a bartender.

G.O.N.Y. (Voice Box)
Like that matters to me, bitch.

WE HEAR the sound of sirens in the background.

G.O.N.Y. (Voice Box) (CONT'D)
Actually you can serve me better alive than dead. You tell the cops you don't know what happened. It was all a blur to you. Do you understand me?

JUSTINE nods her head.

G.O.N.Y. (Voice Box) (CONT'D)
Don't make me regret letting you live.

G.O.N.Y. hesitates for a second. He takes his gun and smashes it over JUSTINE's head. JUSTINE collapses onto the floor right next to MAC.

TIME CUT TO:

EXT. THE LION'S DEN - LATER

The scene is massed with POLICE, AMBULANCES, NEWS CREWS, and nosey SPECTATORS.

JUSTINE sits at the edge of an AMBULANCE with an ice pack on her head. An E.M.T checks her over.

E.M.T.
Everything looks all right, ma'am. We will run some test back at the hospital, but you should be fine.

JUSTINE
Thanks.

KEVIN MALLEY walks up to JUSTINE. He's a sharp-looking guy, green eyes, short black hair, mid-thirties. He's rather tall with very broad shoulders. He flashes his badge to the E.M.T.

KEVIN
(to the E.M.T.)
Detective Malley.
(beat)
How's she doing?

E.M.T.
She should be fine with a couple of days rest.

KEVIN
Mind if I ask her some questions?

E.M.T.
Not if she doesn't.

KEVIN looks at JUSTINE.

KEVIN
Ma'am?

JUSTINE
Sure.

BACK TO:

INT. JUSTINE'S CAR - CONTINUOUS

JUSTINE
The son of a bitch knocked me out cold. But, I did meet Kevin that night.

MAGGIE
Who's Kevin?

JUSTINE
(smiles)
The cutest guy I ever dated. He gave me a ride to the hospital that night and we've been seeing each other ever since.

MAGGIE
So, you know for sure G.o.n.y exists.

JUSTINE
It was the only contact I ever had with him. But right, at least I know he exists and I'm not just wasting my time. We know that he wears a mask and uses something to disguise his voice. Mac had to have seen his face. That's why he had the mask.

MAGGIE
What happened to Mac?

JUSTINE
(smiles)
The tough bastard survived. He's in the hospital now in the coma ward. Very few know where he is and he is under guard at all times. We had a fake funeral for him to rest any suspicious minds. We didn't want G.o.n.y. to know he's still alive.
(beat)
I just hope he comes out of his coma soon, and I hope he can remember what he saw.

MAGGIE
How long ago was that?

JUSTINE
It's been a little over three months now. They shut down Slim's hotel and did an investigation, but came

up flat. No witnesses, no evidence, nothing to link anything together.

(beat)

Slim walked with a slap on the wrist and as far as I know, the Italians gave G.o.n.y. his piece, and the cops closed the case. Something just isn't right, and we're going to set it right! The hotel reopens next Friday. We need to get you a job.

MAGGIE

Right.

(beat)

So you and Mac are really close?

JUSTINE

Like brother and sister. I thought I was going to lose him for sure.

MAGGIE

I know what it's like to lose a brother.

JUSTINE

Anything you would like to talk about?

MAGGIE

My brother Sean died when we were kids.

JUSTINE

Sorry.

MAGGIE glances out of the window for a minute. You can tell she's uncomfortable about talking about SEAN.

MAGGIE

Thanks. It's a long story.

(beat)

So where are we going anyway?

JUSTINE points.

JUSTINE

In there.

P.O.V. MAGGIE:

She sees a Club called "*THE COFFEE SHOP.*"

JUSTINE
This is a local watering hole for Manhattan's elite. We need to start showing you off and get you a job.
(beat)
Have you thought of your alias and back story?

JUSTINE maneuvers her way towards the Valet Parking. A typical underground garage seen in Manhattan. Specifically for the Club. There are a few CARS in front of her.

MAGGIE
I always liked Courtney. Courtney Summers from Chicago.

JUSTINE
Okay, not bad. What brings you to New York, Courtney?

MAGGIE
I want to study film and become an actress. Maybe do Some modeling.

JUSTINE smiles.

JUSTINE
That's perfect. But my suggestion would be to keep the name Maggie. It sounds a little more innocent.
(beat)
How do we know each other?

MAGGIE draws a blank. She cannot come up with an answer right away.

JUSTINE (CONT'D)
It's pauses like that, Maggie, that can give us away. You must be sharp and natural with your answers. Come on, think of something.

MAGGIE
I'm your cousin from Chicago who always dreamed about being on Broadway. We started e-mailing each other and you offered for me to stay with you for a while.

JUSTINE
(smiles)
I like that. I like that a lot.

JUSTINE reaches over into her glove compartment and removes a small BLACK BOX.

MAGGIE
That was going to be my next question. The black box. What did sarge mean?

JUSTINE opens the box.

CLOSE UP:

The BLACK BOX contains little amounts of narcotics. A couple of rolled up joints, some pills, and some cocaine.

MAGGIE (CONT'D)
Whoa, why are you carrying drugs?

JUSTINE
This, Maggie, is the start of your real training.

JUSTINE takes out a SMALL BAGGIE with an ecstasy pill inside. She then closes the box and puts it back inside her glove compartment.

JUSTINE (CONT'D)
Tonight you are not a cop. I want you to experience this full on. No restrictions and no rules. I want you to see how it feels to be on the other side. And I want you to remember everything you can.
(beat)
But most important. Don't ever forget the side you are on. You are a cop and they are the criminals. Learn to maintain and never let the drug affect your actions. Overcome it and use it. Learn to focus under pressure.

MAGGIE's skeptical.

MAGGIE
I don't know about this, Justine.
(beat)
What about drug tests?

JUSTINE
Don't worry about that. Sarge lets us know about the test, besides we are undercover and can bend the rules a little.

JUSTINE pulls up to the VALET, a young, LATIN AMERICAN male. He notices right away whose car it is and perks up.

JUSTINE rolls down her window.

JUAN (Spanish Accent)
Justine! Where have you been? I missed you.

JUSTINE
(smiles)
Juan. How are you? I know I haven't been around. I was out of town visiting some relatives.
(laughs)
I brought back my cousin Maggie from Chicago. Isn't she beautiful?

JUAN smiles.

JUAN (Spanish Accent)
Yes, yes she is beautiful.

MAGGIE
(awkwardly)
Thanks.

JUSTINE
Hey, Juan, can you get me a bottle of water.
(smiles)
I know you always have a cooler with goodies.

JUAN (Spanish Accent)
Sure, anything for you.

JUSTINE rolls up her window.

JUSTINE
It's time I introduced you to all the players.

MAGGIE
(nervously)
I don't know, Justine.

JUAN comes back over with the bottle of water. He taps on the window. JUSTINE rolls it down.

JUAN (Spanish Accent)
Here you go. No charge.

JUSTINE
Thanks, Juan, you're a sweetie. Give me a sec, okay.

JUAN nods, and JUSTINE rolls up her window.

JUSTINE (CONT'D)
You ready?

JUSTINE hands MAGGIE the bottle of water. MAGGIE takes it.

JUSTINE (CONT'D)
Hold out your hand.

MAGGIE holds out her hand and JUSTINE places the pill into her palm.

MAGGIE(V.O.)
I didn't know what I was getting myself into. I was jittery about it, and I was literally shaking from head to toe. All I could think about was Sean. Was this the right thing to do?
(beat)
If it gets me closer to those I could help, why not, right? I didn't know.
(beat)
Then the words just flew out of my mouth.
(beat)
FUCK IT!

MAGGIE slaps the pill into her mouth, unscrews the top of the bottle of water, and swallows it.

JUSTINE
That's my girl. All right, let's go.

JUSTINE and MAGGIE exit the car. JUSTINE hands JUAN a crisp twenty, and JUAN hands her a ticket.

JUSTINE (CONT'D)
Park me in a good spot Juan. No scratches.

JUAN
I already have a spot picked out.

JUAN gets into her car and drives off down into the Garage.

P.O.V. MAGGIE:

She sees the line to get in. It's pretty long.

MAGGIE
What about that line?

JUSTINE
We don't wait on lines.
(grabs Maggie's hand)
C'mon, cuz.

JUSTINE and MAGGIE walk right past the line of PEOPLE and straight up to a big, white doorman named TEDDY.

JUSTINE (CONT'D)
(flirtatiously)
Hey there, Teddy bear.

TEDDY
(smiles big)
Hey there, Justine. Where ya been?

JUSTINE kisses TEDDY on the cheek.

JUSTINE
Busy, busy. Say hi to my cousin Maggie. She's new in town and I'm showing her a good time.

TEDDY
Hello, Maggie. Nice to meet you.

MAGGIE
Nice to meet you, too, Teddy.

TEDDY unhooks the Velvet Ropes.

TEDDY
You two can go right in.

JUSTINE
Thanks, Teddy bear.

The TWO walk in.

TEDDY
Hey, we still have some business to discuss.

He hooks the Velvet Ropes back together.

JUSTINE
I'll call you.

TEDDY
All right. See you later.

INT. THE COFFEE SHOP -- MOVING -- CONTINUOUS

The atmosphere is expensively casual. Looks like an overly big coffee lounge in its decor. Music thumps. Comfortably crowded.

JUSTINE leads MAGGIE through the CLUB-GOERS. JUSTINE mingles in her stride with a few "HELLO"s to some PEOPLE she knows.

MAGGIE
(leans in)
You sure know a lot of people.

JUSTINE pulls in close to give MAGGIE advice.

JUSTINE
It's all part of the game, you'll learn. You never know when you might need a favor.
(beat)
And one of them could be a potential favor, understand?

MAGGIE nods.

JUSTINE (CONT'D)
C'mon. Let's go over here.

JUSTINE takes MAGGIE over to a side bar in the back of the Club.

JUSTINE (CONT'D)
What do you drink?

MAGGIE
I'll take a beer.

JUSTINE
(smiles)
A woman after my own heart.

A MALE BARTENDER struts over. He's good-looking, with a killer smile.

BARTENDER
What can I get you ladies this evening?

JUSTINE
Two buds. No glass.

BARTENDER
Coming right up.

MAGGIE
(jokingly)
Someone you don't know?

JUSTINE
Nope. He must be new.

JUSTINE glances at his butt.

JUSTINE (CONT'D)
I would have remembered that ass.

The TWO laugh.

JUSTINE (CONT'D)
How you feeling?

MAGGIE
I feel fine so far.

The BARTENDER comes back with the drinks.

BARTENDER
That will be twelve.

JUSTINE throws down a twenty.

JUSTINE
Keep it.

BARTENDER
Thanks. I got your next round.

JUSTINE sips her beer and glances around. She scans the Club for anybody and anyone. She finally hones in on the V.I.P. section on the second level.

P.O.V. JUSTINE:

She sees SLIM, LESTER, and SIDNEY. The THREE are having a good time. WOMEN all around.

JUSTINE (O.S.)
All right, cuz, game time.
(leans in)
Take a peek up into the V.I.P.

MAGGIE sips her beer then glances up.

P.O.V. MAGGIE:

She studies THEM intensely.

JUSTINE (O.S.)
Those are the three spirits. The twins are Sidney and Lester Henderson.
(beat)
A.k.a., the Boogey man and the sandman.

MAGGIE (O.S.)
How can you tell them apart?

JUSTINE (O.S.)
You can't. Well, at least I can't.
(beat)
They are G.o.n.y.'s muscle. They are not to be taken lightly. They are both feared and respected.
(beat)
And of course there is Reggie Phillips. A.k.a., Slim . . .
(beat)
a.k.a. the candyman. Slim is as smart as they come and as sneaky as they come. Nothing is sold, sniffed, shot, or injected in his club without him knowing about it.

MAGGIE sips her beer.

MAGGIE
What I don't understand is, why doesn't his so-called competition take them out?

JUSTINE
Because of G.o.n.y.'s reputation. Not to mention hidden identity. No one knows how deep he goes. Who he knows? Who *he* works for? No one knows.
(sarcastically)
And of course that little rumor going around.

MAGGIE
What rumor is that?

JUSTINE
(real serious)
You fuck with G.o.n.y. or his troops, he'll kill your entire family while you watch.

ANGLE ON:

MAGGIE starts to rub her hands together repeatedly.

JUSTINE (CONT'D)
So now we have to figure out a way of getting you a job.

Suddenly hands wrap around JUSTINE's eyes and a MALE VOICE calls out.

MALE VOICE (O.S.)
Guess who?

JUSTINE turns around. She is completely shocked. It is KEVIN MALLEY, her boyfriend.

JUSTINE
Kevin!
(nervous)
What are you doing here?

She kisses him on the lips.

KEVIN
We were out prowling the town. I figured we would stop to see if you were here.
(to Justine)

You remember my partner Patrick?

PATRICK HENNESSY walks out from behind KEVIN. He's tall with a sizable build. He has dirty blond hair and brown eyes. Early thirties with very big dimples.

JUSTINE
Hey, Patrick.
(kisses his cheek)
How are you?

PATRICK
I'm well. Nice to see you again.

KEVIN
And this must be your cousin Maggie you told me about.

JUSTINE opens her eyes wide at MAGGIE.

JUSTINE
Maggie, this is my boyfriend, Kevin.
(wrinkles her forehead)
They are New York City detectives.

MAGGIE is really starting to feel the effects of the drug. KEVIN extends his hand.

KEVIN
Nice to finally meet you.

MAGGIE returns the handshake.

MAGGIE
Nice to meet you.

PATRICK is visibly attracted to MAGGIE immediately. He's quick to introduce himself.

PATRICK
Hi, Maggie, I'm Patrick.

He extends his hand.

MAGGIE
Nice to meet you, Patrick.

MAGGIE returns the handshake but doesn't let loose right away. She starts to rub his hand.

MAGGIE (CONT'D)
Your hands feel nice. Very strong.

PATRICK is taken back a bit.

PATRICK
Thanks.

MAGGIE
So what do you detect?

PATRICK
Murders. We are homicide detectives.

She continues to rub his hand. JUSTINE nonchalantly grabs MAGGIE's hand away.

PATRICK (CONT'D)
So what brings you to New York, Maggie?

MAGGIE
I would love to study film.
(beat)
I always wanted to model, maybe act one day.

PATRICK
Well, you sure are pretty enough to be a model.

MAGGIE brushes her hand against his face.

MAGGIE
Aren't you sweet. Wow, what a smooth face.

KEVIN
(to Justine)
Is she okay?

JUSTINE
She's fine.
(beat)
She's had a few already.

MAGGIE is very loose and relaxed the way JUSTINE wanted her. The arrival of KEVIN and PATRICK was something she didn't see coming.

JUSTINE starts to grow anxious. She keeps eyeing up the V.I.P. to make sure SLIM doesn't notice her.

P.O.V. JUSTINE:

SLIM's no longer up there.

KEVIN and JUSTINE talk. MAGGIE and PATRICK engage in a side conversation.

MAGGIE
So what about you, Patrick? Married, single, girlfriend?

PATRICK
Nope.

MAGGIE
Really, a cute guy like you?

PATRICK
So far. Haven't met Ms. Right yet.
(beat)
What about you?

MAGGIE
I'm single, too.
(beat)
I'm complicated. Most guys don't seem to want complicated.

PATRICK
(smiles)
Maybe you just haven't met the right guy yet. A guy who likes figuring out puzzles, especially complicated ones.

MAGGIE smiles and sips her beer. For the most part she handles the effects of the drug pretty well.

SUDDENLY SLIM's VOICE calls out.

SLIM (V.O.)
Well, well, well. Justine, how are we doing?

JUSTINE's facial expression could stop a train right on its tracks. But she keeps her cool and plays her role.

JUSTINE
Hey, Slim. What's going on?
(beat)
Nice suit.

SLIM tugs on his jacket smugly.

SLIM
Thanks. It's real silk.
(looks at Kevin and Patrick)
Not that fake shit.

JUSTINE walks over and hugs and kisses him on his cheek. SLIM eyes JUSTINE up and down.

SLIM (CONT'D)
Damn baby! You are lookin' fine. Can't wait to get you back behind my bar.
(beat)
Keepin' all my male customers spending that money. Even the married ones . . . mmmmm.

KEVIN gives SLIM a stare.

SLIM (CONT'D)
(cockily)
How are we doing today, officers? Can I buy you a round?

KEVIN
I'm fine.

PATRICK
Not thirsty.

SLIM pulls out a WAD of cash and peels off a hundred dollar bill. He tosses it on the bar.

SLIM
Then I'll leave the tip.
(grins)
No hard feelings about closing me down for almost three months, gentlemen. I know you were just doing your job.

PATRICK
People were murdered. What did you think, asshole. You were going to be open the next day?

SLIM
(arrogantly)
Well, isn't your job to find that kind of element and put them behind bars. I can't control everyone who wants to stay at the Lion's Den and party in the Jungle.
(beat)
Maybe if you took your job more seriously—

PATRICK interrupts and moves towards SLIM.

KEVIN
(angry)
You son of a bitch.

PATRICK angers rather quickly. KEVIN puts his hand on his shoulder.

KEVIN (CONT'D)
Relax, partner. No point in ruining our night. Besides, sooner or later we'll get 'em. Shit always floats to the top.

SLIM
(laughs)
Much later would be my guess, playa.

SLIM turns his attention to MAGGIE.

SLIM (CONT'D)
And who is this red-headed angel standing in front of me?

MAGGIE smiles.

MAGGIE
Hi, I'm Maggie.

SLIM
Maggie. What a beautiful name.

SLIM reaches out his hand for a shake. MAGGIE reaches her hand out in return. SLIM brings it up to his lips and kisses it.

MAGGIE
Thank you.

JUSTINE jumps right in.

JUSTINE
She's my cousin from Chicago. She's going to be staying with me for a while.
(beat)
She's one hell of a bartender Slim.

SLIM looks at JUSTINE then at MAGGIE. SLIM can tell MAGGIE's high on something.

SLIM
Is she really? She looks like a party girl to me. Are you a party girl, little Ms. Maggie from the windy city?

MAGGIE
When it's time to party, I party. When it's time to work, I work.

KEVIN and PATRICK are really aggravated at SLIM's presence.

KEVIN
I think you have worn out your welcome.

SLIM gives KEVIN a mean stare.

PATRICK
I don't remember anyone inviting him in the first place.

JUSTINE
Hey, guys, control your testosterone already.

SLIM
Justine, why don't you bring Maggie down on Friday for our grand reopening. I'll see what I can do about getting her some work.

JUSTINE
Thanks, Slim. I appreciate it.

MAGGIE

I'll be there.

SLIM

You ladies have a good night. If you desire better company, you know where I'll be.

(beat)

Remember, Justine, you're my number one girl now.

He looks at KEVIN and PATRICK and chuckles.

SLIM (CONT'D)

Gentlemen.

SLIM walks (O.S.).

KEVIN

I hate that asshole. I can't believe you want to go back to work for him. Especially after what happened to your friend.

JUSTINE

I'm a bartender, Kevin. He treats me good and pays me well. And even you said yourself it had nothing to do with him.

KEVIN

No, I said I couldn't find any evidence that linked him to the deaths.

JUSTINE

Please, Kevin, don't start with me. Can't we just have a good time tonight?

KEVIN

Sure.

JUSTINE grabs SLIM's hundred from the bar and smiles.

JUSTINE

Come on, drinks are on me.

MAGGIE

I'll take another.

KEVIN and PATRICK loosen up.

KEVIN
All right. All right. I'm in.

PATRICK
(smiles)
Let's drink.

JUSTINE waves to the BARTENDER.

JUSTINE
Hey, Bartender, I need shots.

TIME CUT TO:

INT. THE COFFEE SHOP -- LATER

SMALL CLUB MONTAGE:

We see the four of them dance. Kevin with Justine. Patrick with Maggie.

We see the four of them drink more shots. Maggie is very touchy with Patrick. She stays real close to him. She rubs his shoulders and holds his hand.

We see Justine take notice. She waves over the bartender, who in return brings over a bottle of water. Justine removes Maggie's drink from the bar and gives her the water.

We see them back on the dance floor. They laugh and play and have a good time.

We see Slim watch from the V.I.P. lounge. He watches them closely as he sips a drink. He eyes up Maggie and Patrick especially.

END SMALL CLUB MONTAGE.

SMASH CUT TO:

INT. JUSTINE'S APT. --- MAGGIE'S ROOM -- LATER

MAGGIE and PATRICK kiss in MAGGIE's bed. They are hot and heavy. MAGGIE is on top of PATRICK.

MAGGIE
Oh God you feel so good. I want you so bad.

PATRICK

I want you too.

MAGGIE and PATRICK continue to kiss. Suddenly, in the midst of passion, PATRICK pulls away from MAGGIE.

MAGGIE

What?

(beat)

Why are you stopping?

PATRICK

I . . . I don't know. Maggie, I like you a lot. I really do . . .

(beat)

But . . .

MAGGIE

But? But what? There's no buts.

MAGGIE starts to kiss him again. The drug makes her real aggressive. PATRICK pushes her away and gets up.

He begins to dress.

PATRICK

I want this. I really do.

(beat)

But not like this. You're drunk and I'm drunk.

MAGGIE

So? We are both drunk. Come back to bed and let's sober up.

PATRICK grabs the doorknob.

PATRICK

Not like this, Maggie.

(beat)

I'll call you.

PATRICK opens the door and leaves.

MAGGIE

(frustrated)

Great! Just great!

MAGGIE pulls the sheets over her head and lets out a big "*SIGH.*"

DISSOLVE TO:

INT. JUSTINE'S APT. -- KITCHEN -- MORNING

JUSTINE prances around in sweat pants and a white t-shirt. She mixes some sort of chocolate protein shake.

ENTER MAGGIE. She looks tired and hung over. She makes her way to a Kitchen chair and plops herself down into it.

JUSTINE
Morning . . . cuz.

MAGGIE
Morning.
(holds her head)
Oh, God! I'm never drinking again.

JUSTINE
(laughs)
I say that every weekend.

JUSTINE opens a cabinet and grabs a bottle of aspirin. She opens the bottle and tosses a few aspirin into the chocolate shake. She hits blend on the blender.

MAGGIE grabs her ears from the noise of the blender.

MAGGIE
Oh God, make it stop.

JUSTINE snickers a bit. She stops the blender and grabs a nearby glass and pours the shake inside. She walks it over to MAGGIE and slides it in front of her.

JUSTINE
Drink that. It will make you feel better.

MAGGIE looks down at it then leans over and sniffs it.

MAGGIE
What is it?

JUSTINE
Just drink it. Trust me.

MAGGIE sips it.

MAGGIE
Mmmmm . . . pretty good.

JUSTINE pours herself one as well. She takes a seat down next to MAGGIE.

JUSTINE
How did your night go with Patrick?

MAGGIE wrinkles her nose.

MAGGIE
It's been over a year since I've been with anyone.
(beat)
Finally, when I really want it, he decides to be a gentleman and leaves.

JUSTINE laughs and almost spits out her shake.

JUSTINE
Really?

MAGGIE
Really.

JUSTINE
Why?

MAGGIE
He said he really likes me and maybe we drank too much. He said he wanted to wait.

JUSTINE
Awww, that's so sweet.

MAGGIE
I guess. But I didn't want sweet last night. That drug is intense.

JUSTINE
(smiles)
Yes, it is.
(beat)
You gonna see him again?

MAGGIE
How could I not? He's sweet.

The TWO laugh with each other.

MAGGIE (CONT'D)
Men! I'll never understand them.
(beat)
What about you? How did your night go?

JUSTINE just smirks and sips her drink.

JUSTINE
A lady never tells.

MAGGIE
That good?

JUSTINE
Real good.

WE HEAR a "KNOCK" at the door.

JUSTINE (CONT'D)
I'll get it.

JUSTINE gets up, walks over to the door, and opens it. It's SGT. JACOBS.

She holds a huge cup of coffee in one hand and a thick FILE in the other hand.

JUSTINE (CONT'D)
Morning, sarge. C'mon in.

SGT. JACOBS
Thanks.

She enters and JUSTINE closes the door.

SGT. JACOBS (CONT'D)
How's our girl doing?

JUSTINE
Hung over to say the least.
(beat)

But, with a twist of strange luck, I think I got her a job. Friday night we go back into the jungle.

SGT. JACOBS
(smiles)
Good. That's good news.

The TWO enter the Kitchen.

SGT. JACOBS (CONT'D)
Hey there, Ms. Maggie May.

MAGGIE
Morning, sarge.

P.O.V. MAGGIE:

She sees that SGT. JACOBS has on her sneakers again.

MAGGIE
Feet hurt?

SGT. JACOBS
Like you wouldn't believe.

MAGGIE smiles.

JUSTINE
I introduced her to all the players and she even got to meet Kevin and Patrick, our resident homicide detectives.
(beat)
I think Patrick has taken to her.

SGT. JACOBS takes a seat and places her FILE on the kitchen table.

SGT. JACOBS
Really? That's good. Now, both of you can keep an eye on them.

MAGGIE
An eye? What does that mean?

SGT. JACOBS
Yeah, an eye. The more information you can get from them and give to me, the more it will help us.

JUSTINE
Speaking of information.
(beat)
How did the investigation go? I know you said you had a friend that was gonna dig a little deeper into their records than what we already got.

SGT. JACOBS sips her coffee.

SGT. JACOBS
My contact found out nothing on them. As far as I know, they are clean. They just have no luck, like us. The hotel massacre, came up empty. The same with the Triads warehouse. They have no evidence linking G.o.n.y. or Slim to any of those homicides.
(beat)
It seems all the evidence either disappears or isn't solid enough to further their investigations. They're just as stumped as we are.

SGT. JACOBS makes a face at the TWO.

JUSTINE
What? You suspect a mole?

SGT. JACOBS
What do you think? This fucking G.o.n.y. character is really starting to piss me off.

JUSTINE
Our cover isn't blown, is it?

MAGGIE breaks out of her hang over and interjects.

MAGGIE
Wait, hold on a minute.
(to Justine)
You're fucking Kevin to get information out of him?

JUSTINE looks over at SGT. JACOBS.

JUSTINE
Yes and no. I mean I really like him, and if he can help, why not? I get the best of both worlds. Any info I get from him I give to sarge.

MAGGIE
So you think I'm going to do the same thing to Patrick? Use him?

SGT. JACOBS
Let me tell you something, Maggie. You better thicken that pretty little skin of yours. This isn't a game you win or lose. In this game, if you lose, you can die. Anybody and anything around you is a tool.
(beat)
You use that tool to its full extent. We have gotten deep, real deep, and I will be damned if Mac is going to be laid up in a hospital holding onto his life for nothing. If this is too much for you, you let us know right now.
(beat)
And *no,* Justine, to answer your question. Your cover has not been blown. I am the only one that knows about you two. And I plan on keeping it that way. I don't want to hospitalize any more of my agents or bury them either.
(to Maggie)
Is this too much for you?

MAGGIE
No, no, I'm not saying I can't handle it. I just don't want to hurt Patrick.

SGT. JACOBS
He will be fine. If he happens to confide in you and opens up, great. Maybe he'll tell you a few things that can help us. What's the harm in that?

MAGGIE nods her head and sips her shake.

SGT. JACOBS (CONT'D)
So, how did Slim take to our redhead?

JUSTINE
He likes her. I could tell. Not to mention she was a little . . .
(smiles)
touchy touchy if you can catch my drift.

SGT. JACOBS smiles at MAGGIE.

SGT. JACOBS
Really?
(to Maggie)
You asked Vanna for a vowel? A little "E" for your puzzle. How was that?

MAGGIE gives a guilty pleasure glance to SGT. JACOBS.

MAGGIE
I'm not gonna lie. It was one of the best nights of my life.

SGT. JACOBS
Can you remember the night, is the important thing?

MAGGIE
I remember everything. It feels like it's tattooed into my memory. The sounds, the voices, the smells.
(beat)
The Boogeyman, the Sandman, the Candyman, all of it.

SGT. JACOBS
Good.

SGT. JACOBS opens up the FILE on the table and takes a big sip of her coffee.

SGT. JACOBS (CONT'D)
Now let's get to work and bring you up to speed on how G.o.n.y. and Slim's operation works.

DISSOLVE TO:

INT. THE JUNGLE -- SLIM'S CLUB - NIGHT

G.O.N.Y.'s OPERATION MONTAGE.

THE CAMERA FOLLOWS ALL ACTION OVER SGT. JACOBS VOICE OVER.

The club is crowed. Music thumps.

JUSTINE work behind the main bar. They wear their usual WHITE t-shirts. The CAMERA PANS to the side bar. WE RECOGNIZE CARA and DEBBIE in their RED and BLUE t-shirts.

Other BARTENDERs mill about. ALL wear different colored t-shirts. GREEN, PINK, and YELLOW.

WE FOCUS on JUSTINE. She fixes drinks and works the register.

SGT. JACOBS (V.O.)
Slim is as careful as he is dangerous. He's like a mad scientist. He has workers working the club at all times. All of them wear different colored shirts. To the blind eye, they seem like work uniforms, but in retrospect mean different things.
(beat)
Example, white shirts mean cocaine. Red shirts mean heroin, green shirts mean weed, and yellow deals with ice or methadone. Blue is crack, and let's not forget your favorite—the pink shirts which mean ecstasy. Each bartender is responsible for his or her own orders.
(beat)
The Lion's Den is a high-class hotel, catering to numerous high rollers. Hip-Hop artists, rock stars, actors and actresses. They come from all around to party in the Jungle. I'm sure Justine explained that to you already.

ANGLE ON:

A famous HIP-HOP ARTIST enters the club. FANS swarm as he walks through the door with TWO WOMEN by his side. Money gleams off this artist from his jewelry to his clothes.

SLIM greets the Hip-Hop ARTIST with open arms. They shake hands and hug. The TWINS readily come over and escort the ARTIST to the V.I.P. section.

SGT. JACOBS (V.O.) (CONT'D)
Now what transpires from there is the genius part of the equation.

WE SEE the ARTIST party with his TWO WOMEN. THEY drink and drink, running up the tab. All types of high-end liquor.

SGT. JACOBS (V.O.) CONT'D)
When a star or high profile guest gets in the mood for a little something extra, they must go through a process.

The ARTIST leans in to one of his WOMEN and gives her a WAD of cash. She kisses his cheek and makes her way over to JUSTINE.

SGT. JACOBS (V.O.) (CONT'D)
They simply lean in to the bartender's ear and whisper for their room to be blessed.

WE READ THE WOMAN's LIPS.

WOMAN
Bartender, please bless Penthouse M.

The WOMAN slides JUSTINE the money.

JUSTINE takes the money and walks over to a cooler. She reaches into the cooler for a bottle of water. Carefully, she counts the money while she reaches inside the cooler. She walks back over to the Woman and gives her the bottle of water.

WE READ JUSTINE's LIPS.

JUSTINE
Penthouse M will be blessed shortly.

The woman takes the water and heads back to her party.

SGT. JACOBS (V.O.)
The monies exchanged are then taken into the kitchen.
(beat)
Of course the Lion's Den has room service. The guests must eat.

JUSTINE makes her way into the Kitchen. She passes by CHEFs, COOKs, and DISHWASHERS. They pay her no mind. She maneuvers quickly by them and walks up to a WALK-IN FREEZER.

She ENTERS it.

INT. WALK IN FREEZER - CONTINUOUS

Inside the freezer is all types of FROZEN FOOD.

JUSTINE makes her way to the back of the freezer. She stands in front of a MEAT RACK. She reaches her foot underneath the meat rack and steps on a TILE.

SGT. JACOBS (V.O.)
When the tile is stepped on, it locks the freezer door from the inside. No one may enter while an order is being placed.

P.O.V. JUSTINE:

She turns to look up at a SMALL CAMERA in the corner of the Walk In Freezer and signals.

CUT TO:

INT. SECRET ROOM - MOMENTS LATER

WE SEE a VIDEO MONITOR with JUSTINE's image on it.

SGT. JACOBS (V.O.)
There is a secret room in the back behind the wall of frozen foods. Inside the room are six workers.

Inside WE SEE the SIX WORKERs. TWO ARMED BODYGUARDs, THREE HIVE WORKERs, and a COUNTER.

The TWO BODYGUARDs stand nearest the secret wall.

BODYGUARD ONE checks the Video Monitor on a LAPTOP. He recognizes JUSTINE and signals BODYGUARD TWO.

BODYGUARD TWO punches in a CODE on a nearby DIGITAL KEYPAD on the inside of the room.

CUT TO:

INT. WALK IN FREEZER - MOMENTS LATER

WE SEE a "RACK OF LAMB" that appears to be real fold down. JUSTINE reaches in and hands BODYGUARD TWO the money.

BODYGUARD TWO
Order number? Shirt color? Order?

JUSTINE
Penthouse M. White. Two balls.

BODYGUARD TWO
Confirming order.

BODYGUARD TWO hands the money over to the COUNTER.

COUNTER
Shirt color?

BODYGUARD TWO
White.

The COUNTER counts the money and confirms the order. He signals the HIVE WORKERs.

COUNTER
Send two balls to Penthouse M.

Deeper inside the Secret Room is a MAIL ROOM where the HIVE WORKERs work. Each room number and penthouse letter with its own round CUBBY SLOT. The HIVE WORKERs work their own chosen cubby slots.

The HIVE WORKER who works the Penthouse section gets up and walks over to a BEER COOLER. She opens it.

CLOSE UP:

Inside the beer cooler is every drug imaginable, all pre-bagged and ready for distributing. She grabs TWO EIGHTBALLs of cocaine and closes the cooler.

Inside each cubby slot is a ROUND PLASTIC CONTAINER.

SGT. JACOBS (V.O.)
The containers they use are like the ones at the bank. A vacuum system of sorts. Like a funnel. Real fucking genius if you ask me.

The HIVE WORKER places the order inside the container and the container back into the cubby slot. She hits a button next to her designated cubby slot and sends the container.

CAMERA FOLLOWS THE PLASTIC CONTAINER THROUGH THE WALLS OF THE HOTEL UNTIL FINALLY IT STOPS.

The COUNTER then checks a LOG BOOK and writes NUMBERS down on a piece of paper and hands it over to BODYGUARD TWO.

BODYGUARD TWO takes the paper over to JUSTINE and gives it to her. He punches in another CODE on the digital keypad and the "RACK OF LAMB" closes over. He signals BODYGUARD ONE.

BODYGUARD ONE punches in a CODE himself on his LAPTOP, which releases the lock on the walk in box door.

JUSTINE takes the piece of paper back outside to the bar.

INT. THE JUNGLE -- SLIM'S CLUB - MOMENTS LATER

JUSTINE signals the WOMAN. THE WOMAN gets up and walks over to JUSTINE. JUSTINE slips her the piece of paper.
WE READ JUSTINE's LIPS.

JUSTINE
Penthouse M has been blessed.

CUT TO:

INT. PENTHOUSE M - MOMENTS LATER

The HIP-HOP ARTIST stands in front of a DIGITAL SAFE. He opens up the piece of paper that JUSTINE gave to the WOMAN.

ANGLE ON:

On the paper is a combination that reads: 23--24--42

He punches in the CODE and the safe door opens. He removes the ROUND PLASTIC CONTAINER and takes his order. He then places the piece of paper back inside the container and closes the safe door.

BACK TO:

INT. JUSTINE'S APT. -- KITCHEN - CONTINUOUS

SGT. JACOBS
The combination goes back to the hive workers, who destroy it. Same with the secret room. All of it is attached to a fail-safe system. If the shit hits the fan, the Counter is instructed to blow it.

MAGGIE
Blow it?

JUSTINE
The room is wired with C-4. If the Counter activates the count down sequence, the place goes, kaploowie.

MAGGIE
What a about all that money?

SGT. JACOBS
(beat)
The money as we know it is filtered back into the hotel and the club. Payroll, expenses, construction you name it. Laundered perfectly.
(beat)
Slim has the handle on the entire system and runs it perfectly. But I am positive it is G.o.n.y.'s the brain child. The mastermind himself.

MAGGIE
So what's the plan?

SGT. JACOBS
We get you in there to back up Justine and wait for G.o.n.y. to show his face.

MAGGIE
How do you know G.o.n.y. will show his face?

SGT. JACOBS
We don't. We continue to build our case and wait for an opening.
(to Justine)
Friday, you said?

JUSTINE nods.

SGT. JACOBS (CONT'D)
Then Friday we start all over again.

MAGGIE
What are we suppose to do until Friday?

SGT. JACOBS
Go out and have some fun. Go show your face around the city and learn the streets.

JUSTINE smiles.

JUSTINE
I know two good-looking guys that would love to take us out on the town.

MAGGIE smiles back at JUSTINE.

MAGGIE
Okay, why not? But no more vowels.

The THREE laugh.

DISSOLVE TO:

INT. JUSTINE'S APT. --- MAGGIE'S ROOM - AFTERNOON

MAGGIE puts on a nice outfit.

MAGGIE (V.O.)
I had never gotten to see what New York City had to offer. So I took sarge's advice and had some fun.

MAGGIE AND JUSTINE PAINT THE TOWN MONTAGE.

We see the four of them on a boat. They cruise Manhattan Harbor.

We see the four of them in Little Italy having dinner. They laugh, eat, and drink wine.

We see the four of them stroll down Broadway. Broadway is packed. Maggie's eyes absorb everything.

We see the four of them on top of the Empire State building. Maggie's nervous to look over the railing. Justine playfully pretends to push her over. The two smile and laugh with each other.

We see Maggie lay flowers at Ground Zero. She does the sign of the cross.

We see the four attend a popular Broadway musical. Maggie's eyes are glued to the stage. Patrick smiles and slides his hand over. Maggie looks back at him with a smile and embraces his hand.

We see the four out dancing and drinking.

We see Maggie and Patrick back in Maggie's room. This time it is perfect. They lay back on the bed and make love.

FADE OUT:

FADE IN:

INT. ABANDONED WAREHOUSE - NIGHT

A LONE PERSON sits tied to a chair in the center of the Warehouse. A black hood covers their head.

The sounds of whimpering echoes throughout the blackness of the Warehouse.

ANGLE ON:

Big, black boots smash the ground. They approach the restrained individual.

CAMERA PANS up to REVEAL G.O.N.Y. He stops in front of the LONE PERSON and lifts off the black hood.

Underneath the hood is a beautiful young woman in her early twenties. She has black hair and brown eyes. She is gagged, and her make-up has smudged all over her face from crying.

G.O.N.Y. (Voice Box)

I bet you are wondering what in the world did you do to deserve this.

The GIRL whimpers.

G.O.N.Y. reaches over and brushes her hair away from her face.

G.O.N.Y. (Voice Box) (CONT'D)

Shhh, don't cry, my dear. It will all be over shortly. I promise you that.

(beat)

A simple partnership is all I desired. And now I have to reinforce my threats on you. Poor baby. Not your fault. You just happen to be the wrong daughter of the wrong man.

G.O.N.Y. turns around to the darkness of the Warehouse.

G.O.N.Y. (Voice Box) (CONT'D)

(yells)

BRING HIM TO ME!

Out of the darkness of the Warehouse, the TWINS appear. In their clutches is an older gentleman by the name of IVAN. He is gagged as well. His face bleeds from fresh wounds.

SLIM follows in from behind the THREE. A razor sharp KNIFE dangles in his left hand.

At the sight of the GIRL in the chair, IVAN becomes frantic. He loses control. He tries to free himself from the TWINS' clutches. The TWINS are too strong.

G.O.N.Y. (Voice Box) (CONT'D)
You better behave yourself, Ivan. Or there is no telling what I might do.

The TWINS force IVAN to his knees. The GIRL starts to whimper louder at the sight of IVAN.

G.O.N.Y. (Voice Box) (CONT'D)
Remove his gag.

One of the TWINS pulls off IVAN's gag.

G.O.N.Y. (Voice Box) (CONT'D)
Awww, there is nothing more special than a reunion between father and daughter. I believe she is your first born?

IVAN (Russian Accent)
Please no, I beg you.

SLIM nears G.O.N.Y. and hands him the knife.

G.O.N.Y. (Voice Box)
Beg me? Ivan, it is too late for begging.

IVAN (Russian Accent)
Please, I'll give you everything I have. All of it is yours. Please don't hurt her.

G.O.N.Y. (Voice Box)
Slim, would you please shut him up. There is nothing worse than a beggar.

SLIM
My pleasure.

SLIM walks over to IVAN and ties his gag back around his mouth. He then gives him a hard hit to his chin.

IVAN's face splits even more. Blood spews excessively from his nose. IVAN looks up at SLIM and tries to lunge at him. But the TWINS' grip is relentless.

G.O.N.Y. (Voice Box)
Now, that's better.
(beat)
I have had my problems throughout my time with certain individuals in our so called line of work . . .
(beat)
but none as nearly as stubborn as you Russians. You people, I gotta say, are worthy adversaries. But not smart negotiators.
(beat)
You turned your back on my offers, my associates, and my outright demands, knowing what I would do if they were not met. To me that is a blatant disrespect.
(beat)
Or you thought I was bluffing. Either way, you are mistaken.

G.O.N.Y. takes the knife, pulls back the GIRL's head by her hair, and slices her throat in one motion. Her eyes roll into the back of her head and her head slumps over. Her blood soaks the front of her shirt.

IVAN's eyes glaze over with tears. He bellows loud with grief.

G.O.N.Y. (Voice Box) (CONT'D)
You pay me on Friday.
(thinks)
Seven hundred and fifty thousand dollars for your belligerence. It would have been a million, but I took off a quarter million for your oldest daughter's life. Seems fair to me.
(beat)
After you pay your debt to me, we will discuss other arrangements.

G.O.N.Y. wipes the knife clean on the GIRL's shirt. He hands the knife to SLIM.

G.O.N.Y. (Voice Box) (CONT'D)
Get rid of it.

SLIM nods. The TWINS let IVAN go. He's stricken with grief and can hardly stand.

G.O.N.Y. (Voice Box) (CONT'D)
This Friday, Ivan. You hear me?
(beat)
Or do I have to do the same to your other two daughters and your wife?

IVAN crawls to the feet of his daughter and tries to pull himself up. Tears stream down his face.

G.O.N.Y. (Voice Box) (CONT'D)
Pathetic.
(to his crew)
Let's go!
(to Ivan)
FRIDAY. THE JUNGLE! YOU PAY SLIM. UNDERSTAND?

IVAN (Russian Accent)
(cries)
Yes, yes!

DISSOLVE TO:

INT. THE JUNGLE -- SLIM'S CLUB - NIGHT

SUPERIMPOSE ON SCREEN -- FRIDAY

The club is very crowded. A D.J. PLAYS MUSIC in the background.

The other BARTENDERs go about their business.

MAGGIE works the main bar with JUSTINE. She wears a BLACK SHIRT and JUSTINE wears her WHITE. They're busy. They serve drinks and collect money.

JUSTINE
You know you are wearing a black shirt because Slim doesn't trust you yet.

MAGGIE
I understand.

JUSTINE
Speak of the devil.

SLIM slides over smoothly to the bar. He's dressed to kill as usual.

SLIM
(to Justine)
How's my new girl doing?

JUSTINE
Good. Showing her the ropes, and I introduced her to the crew. Debbie, Cara, and the others.

JUSTINE leans over to a CUSTOMER.

JUSTINE (CONT'D)
What can I get you?

SLIM leans over to MAGGIE.

SLIM
So, what do you think, Maggie? You gonna join our family?

MAGGIE
Sure, as long as there is money to be made.

SLIM
Don't you worry about that, kitten.
(winks at her)
There's always ways to make money.

The TWINS walk into FRAME, all business. LESTER leans into SLIM's ear with a secretive comment. SIDNEY stands behind LESTER.

P.O.V. SLIM: - MOMENTS LATER

He looks to the front entrance and sees IVAN enter.

SLIM (O.S.)
(cockily)
See, Maggie. There's always ways to make money.

Suddenly, SIX RUSSIAN HITMEN push their way in through the entrance with SLIM's DOORMAN in their clutches. The DOORMAN drops to the floor next to IVAN. His neck bleeds profusely.

IVAN gives SLIM an evil smile.

SLIM (O.S.) (CONT'D)
(shouts)
SHIT! IT'S A HIT!

THE JUNGLE SHOOT OUT MONTAGE.

We see the Six Russians spread out into an attack formation. All Six reveal automatic weapons hidden inside their suit jackets. They take aim and begin to spray the club with a fury of gunfire. The D.J. booth is their first target. The D.J. catches the bulk of frenzy of bullets. The booth explodes with sparks and smoke. The music stops.

We hear screams and cries.

We see Justine grab Maggie. They duck behind the bar.

We see random club patrons and club workers scatter for cover. Debbie and Cara are not so lucky. Bullets splatter into them fatally.

We see Slim remove his nine millimeters and return fire. He is on the move and his shots aren't precise.

We see the Twins remove their weapons and run for cover. They fire random shots unsuccessfully.

We see the Six Russians spread out and take cover anywhere they can.

We see the enraged Ivan head for Slim, gun in hand. He fires round after round. His shots just miss. Slim slides across Debbie and Cara's side bar just in time. Bullets ricochet off the top of the bar.

We see Justine and Maggie crouched behind the main bar. Justine lifts up her pant leg and removes a .38 from her ankle holster. Maggie gives Justine a worried look.

MAGGIE
I didn't bring my gun. You told me not to!

Bullets whistle through the air. Bottles and debris explode over THEIR heads. The sound is deafening.

JUSTINE

Sorry, here!

JUSTINE quickly tosses MAGGIE her .38.

JUSTINE (CONT'D)

Catch. Cover me!

MAGGIE snatches the .38 out of the air and JUSTINE slowly walks her way towards the cash register. She slides her arm underneath it and removes a panel. Hidden behind the panel is another .38. She leans her back against the bar.

JUSTINE (CONT'D)

Don't get involved unless it's absolutely necessary.

MAGGIE nods her head.

We see Lester fire a clean shot. It slams into one of the Russian Hitmen. He tumbles backwards and falls to the ground dead.

We see Ivan ducked behind some turned-over tables. He continues his fire fight with Slim. Slim is pinned behind the side bar. He waits for opportunities and fires back at Ivan. Both nearly hitting each other.

We see Sidney makes his way fleetly across the dance floor. He fires in his stride. He nails a Russian Hitman with an accurate shot. The Russian catches the bullet in his chest, which propels him into the air. He crashes hard through a nearby glass table.

We see Lester fire his gun. It jams. He fumbles with it and tries to change the clip. Two of the Russians move in quickly. They aim and spray Lester with full clips. Lester wiggles from side to side from the impact of numerous shots. He falls to the ground dead. His eyes still open.

We see Sidney look over at his brother. He stares into his dead eyes and flips out. He runs at the two Russians like an animal. One of the Russians gets off a shot. It hits Sidney in his shoulder, but doesn't faze him.

Sidney charges in like a rhino and barrels into the two Russians. They fall to the ground, hard. Sidney reaches down in the same breath and snaps the neck of the closest Russian. He then turns his fury on the other. The Russian leaps up and swings, but Sidney tackles him right to the ground. They roll around on the ground. Sidney looks up and notices that a Gazelle head is about to fall off its mount. The head falls and tumbles towards the two. Sidney pushes the Russian off of him and rolls out of the way. The Russian looks up and is impaled in his chest by the horns of the Gazelle.

We see and recognize the two Bodyguards from the secret room. They hustle out of the kitchen, guns hot. The hive workers follow behind them, scampering for cover. The Bookkeeper follows behind the hive workers. Laptop and logs in his clutches.

JUSTINE recognizes him. She knows he is a most vital part of the case. He mustn't get away.

He bails out of the kitchen like a rabbit. JUSTINE readily takes aim and plants a shot in his leg.

The BOOKKEEPER tumbles to the ground in pain. The logs and laptop fall out of his grasp.

JUSTINE (CONT'D)
(to Maggie)
Don't let him go. We need that evidence.

MAGGIE sticks her gun in her belt. She moves swiftly and pounces on him like a hungry lion.

He whales in pain.

BOOKKEEPER
My leg, my leg. Oh god, I'm gonna die.
(scared)
Let me go! Let me go!

MAGGIE wrestles with his arms to gain control of him.

MAGGIE
You're not going to die. But you are going to jail.

BOOKKEEPER
Good. Jail is good. Take me! Take me to jail now!

JUSTINE rapidly scoops up the log book and laptop. She places them inside the icy beer cooler and closes over the top. She hustles over to MAGGIE and assists her.

JUSTINE
Good job.

BOOKKEEPER
Let me go! Let me go! The place is going to blow.

MAGGIE
WHAT!

JUSTINE
(nervously)
You set the timer in the back room?

BOOKKEEPER
Yes, yes. We gotta go, now!

JUSTINE
Shit. How much time we have?

BOOKKEEPER
Ten minutes, if that. It's ticking.

JUSTINE
Give me the password to shut it down.

BOOKKEEPER
I can't. G.o.n.y. would kill me and my family if he found out. No way.

MAGGIE
Don't be stupid. We will all die if that bomb goes off.

BOOKKEEPER
I can't. You don't understand.

JUSTINE turns to the beer cooler and opens it. Her mind races. She grabs the log book and places her gun on the cooler.

JUSTINE
Maybe there is a code in here.

The BOOKKEEPER unexpectedly rages with a surge of adrenaline. He pushes MAGGIE away and pulls himself up.

Without warning, a RUSSIAN HITMAN cranes his neck over the bar. He sees three easy targets. His first target is the BOOKKEEPER.

He fires his weapon mercilessly. A barrage of bullets rip through the BOOKKEEPER's chest. He is propelled backwards and lands on MAGGIE. She is thrown to her back. Her gun slips out of her hand.

The RUSSIAN pivots slight left for unsuspecting JUSTINE. MAGGIE stretches out her hand desperately for her gun. Her fingertips touch the hand grip.

MAGGIE
(yells)
JUSTINE!

SLOW MOTION.

JUSTINE turns to see the RUSSIAN. She looks to her left to where her gun is. She reaches over to grab for it.

The RUSSIAN now has his sights on JUSTINE. She grips her gun and tries to beat the RUSSIAN to the draw.

Suddenly, TWO shots rip through the RUSSIAN's chest just before he fires. His eyes roll over white. He drops dead out of view of MAGGIE and JUSTINE.

JUSTINE glances over at MAGGIE. MAGGIE holds the smoking gun in her grasp. Her face drawn and empty.

BACK TO REGULAR MOTION.

Within no time, JUSTINE rushes over and grabs MAGGIE by the wrist. She forcefully pulls her up onto her feet.

JUSTINE
Come on.

The TWO race into the kitchen.

We see Ivan inch his way closer to Slim. Then the two Bodyguards catch Ivan in their sights. They rush out into open view. They fire at Ivan, who has secured himself behind a pillar. They unload their weapons, hoping to hit Ivan. They fail. Ivan loads a fresh clip while the bullets bounce off the pillar. He waits patiently and then springs out away from the pillar, his weapon hot. He pulls the trigger with surgical precision. The bodyguards are hit in the head with two clean shots. They BOTH drop to the ground.

We see Slim pick his moment. He wiggles his way around the bar and notices Ivan's blindside. Slim slides out to the left and takes aim for Ivan's back. Ivan readily spins back around, but Slim fires.

ANGLE ON IVAN:

He takes two shots to his stomach. He steps backwards about three feet. He looks down at his blood. He angers violently. He raises his weapon and walks angrily at SLIM. SLIM takes cover quickly.

IVAN fires, but his shots are way off. His gun then clicks. It's out of ammo. He continues to pull the trigger at SLIM, who stands up from his cover and smiles.

SLIM
(wickedly)
Give my regards to your daughter.

IVAN (Russian Accent)
I will have my revenge in the next life.

SLIM fires one clean shot into IVAN's chest. IVAN falls to his knees and then forward onto his face.

SLIM
I don't think so.

END THE JUNGLE SHOOT OUT MONTAGE.

Suddenly, DOZENs of NYPD, S.W.A.T., and POLICE OFFICERS dart through the entrance, weapons hot.

ALL are in full protective gear ready to kick ass. THEY race to take tactical positions and secure the room.

LEAD S.W.A.T. OFFICER
FREEZE. NOBODY FUCKING BREATHE!

SIDNEY kneels next to his brother. LESTER's head cradled in his arms. His eyes water with tears. He glances up at the POLICE with pure hatred.

P.O.V. SIDNEY:

Sees his brother's gun still grasped in his dead hand. Without hesitation, SIDNEY takes his gun and raises to his feet like a possessed demon.

LEAD S.W.A.T. OFFICER
I said don't move. Drop your weapon.

SIDNEY boldly lifts the gun and fires without care. He walks towards the POLICE with rage. His bullets fling through the air and hit TWO OFFICERS savagely.

LEAD S.W.A.T. OFFICER (CONT'D)
DROP HIM!

The POLICE OFFICERS open fire without mercy.

SIDNEY is brutally shot at close range. Hit over a dozen times before he falls to the floor. His gun still in his grasp.

LEAD S.W.A.T. OFFICER (CONT'D)
Who's next?

SLIM quickly drops his weapons and puts up his hands.

SLIM
(cowardly)
I was just defending myself, officer.

CUT TO:

INT. SECRET ROOM - MOMENTS LATER

MAGGIE and JUSTINE scamper around the room in search of the bomb.

MAGGIE notices a RED WIRE connected to the BEER COOLER where the drugs are stored. She flips open the top and finds the bomb rigged on the inside.

MAGGIE
Found it.

JUSTINE hustles over. She reaches behind the bomb and follows the RED WIRE up out of the BEER COOLER. She looks up into the ceiling and sees huge bricks of C-4.

ANGLE ON:

The TIMER on the bomb reads: 6 minutes.

JUSTINE
Shit! Shit! There's enough C-4 in here to level the hotel.

MAGGIE
What do we do?

ANGLE ON:

The TIMER now reads: 4 minutes and 30 seconds.

JUSTINE
Shit! There's no time to call in the bomb squad.

ANGLE ON:

The TIMER now reads: 4 minutes.

JUSTINE (CONT'D)
We have to do something or a lot of people are going to die.

MAGGIE
Including us and our evidence.

JUSTINE
Right!
(beat)
Well, what do we know?

The TWO study the bomb on the inside of the cooler. The bomb has a GREEN WIRE, a YELLOW WIRE, and a BLUE WIRE attached to it.

MAGGIE
One of those wires has to defuse it, right? One of them has to be the ground.

JUSTINE
Right! Are you sure?

MAGGIE
I think so.

JUSTINE
Okay, which one?

MAGGIE
That I'm not sure about.

ANGLE ON:

The TIMER now reads: 2 minutes and 30 seconds.

JUSTINE reaches into her bar apron and removes a LEMON SHUCKER. She hands it to MAGGIE.

JUSTINE
Here. You cut the wire.

MAGGIE takes it.

MAGGIE
Why me?

JUSTINE holds out her HAND. It shakes uncontrollably.

JUSTINE
My hand's shaking. I'm nervous. I don't want to slip.

ANGLE ON:

The TIMER now reads: 1 minute and 30 seconds.

JUSTINE (CONT'D)
Hurry.

MAGGIE leans over the wires.

MAGGIE
Which one? Which one?

Sweat drips from MAGGIE's brow.

MAGGIE (CONT'D)
I don't know. I don't know.

MAGGIE reaches in to cut a wire. She rotates between wires, not knowing which one to cut.

ANGLE ON:

The TIMER now reads: 10 seconds.

JUSTINE
Oh God. You have to pick one.

MAGGIE moves the SHUCKER to the BLUE WIRE, then changes her mind and moves it to the GREEN WIRE. Sweat pores from her forehead.

MAGGIE
FUCK IT!

MAGGIE cuts the GREEN WIRE.

ANGLE ON:

The TIMER stops with 1 second left.

JUSTINE
Holy shit, you did it. Why did you choose green?

MAGGIE gasps with a sigh of relief.

MAGGIE
The luck of the Irish.

WE HEAR BAGPIPES PLAY OVER THE SCENE.

The TWO hug each other happily.

Suddenly, SEVERAL POLICE OFFICERs enter, gun's drawn.

POLICE OFFICER
FREEZE, YOU TWO. DON'T MOVE.

MAGGIE and JUSTINE startle a bit.

POLICE OFFICER (CONT'D)
(to Maggie)
YOU! DROP THE KNIFE.

MAGGIE
It's not a knife. And lower your weapons we are D—

JUSTINE grabs MAGGIE's arm and shakes her head.

JUSTINE
(mouths it to Maggie)
Don't break our cover.

MAGGIE drops the LEMON SHUCKER.

The POLICE OFFICERs rush in to arrest MAGGIE and JUSTINE.

FADE OUT:

FADE IN:

EXT. THE LION'S DEN - LATER

The street is massed with POLICE CARS, AMBULANCES, S.W.A.T. TRUCKS, and a BOMB SQUAD UNIT. YELLOW POLICE TAPE stretches around the entire crime scene.

Numerous POLICE OFFICERs struggle with NEWS CREWS and nosey SPECTATORS.

KEVIN and PATRICK are on the scene. THEY maneuver about, trying to make sense of the mess.

WE MOVE to MAGGIE and JUSTINE. The TWO are handcuffed in the back of a SQUAD CAR.

THEY sit quietly.

INT. SQUAD CAR - CONTINUOUS

JUSTINE
I never thanked you.

MAGGIE
Thanked me for what?

JUSTINE
For saving my life.
(beat)
Thank you.

MAGGIE sits quietly.

JUSTINE (CONT'D)
What's wrong?

MAGGIE
That's the first time I ever shot anyone.

JUSTINE
It was him or us, Maggie. He would have killed the both of us. I'm glad you didn't hesitate.
(beat)
Or I wouldn't have been able to thank you.

JUSTINE nudges MAGGIE with her shoulder playfully.

MAGGIE
I never really got to tell you why I became an agent.

JUSTINE
No, but I figured you'd tell me when you were ready.
(beat)
If you want, my ears are open now.

MAGGIE
I told you I lost my brother Sean when I was a kid.

JUSTINE
Yeah, I remember.

MAGGIE
I was just ten years old when it happened. I watched him die from a heroin overdose.
(beat)
He died right in front of me, right in my arms. A night I will never forget.

JUSTINE
(condolingly)
I'm sorry, Maggie.

MAGGIE
It tore my family apart. And what made it worse was the son of a bitch that dealt him the drugs never did a minute of time. Got off on some sort of technicality.
(beat)
He moved away shortly after that and no one ever heard from him again. I vowed to myself from that moment on I would try and stop any family anywhere from feeling that pain.
(beat)
The one thing I remember about that bastard was his football jersey number. *Number fifty-two*! That's all I

ever see. ***Fifty-two***! Every time I bust some scumbag lowlife I keep count. I will put fifty-two criminals away in memory of my brother Sean. And I will save fifty-two families from feeling the pain that my family and I went through.

JUSTINE stares at MAGGIE. Her story both inspiring and heartbreaking.

JUSTINE
I'm so sorry, Maggie.

MAGGIE
Don't be sorry for me. Be sorry for my brother Sean who never got to see eighteen.

P.O.V. JUSTINE:

She sees SGT. JACOBS walk onto the crime scene with numerous DEA FIELD AGENTS behind her.

JUSTINE (O.S.)
Jacobs is here.

EXT. THE LION'S DEN - MOMENTS LATER

She walks up to the nearest POLICE OFFICER and flashes her badge.

SGT. JACOBS
Who's in charge?

The POLICE OFFICER points towards KEVIN and PATRICK.

SGT. JACOBS (CONT'D)
(to her Field Agents)
Come on, men!

SGT. JACOBS moves quickly towards KEVIN and PATRICK.

SGT. JACOBS (CONT'D)
(to Kevin)
I was told you were in charge.

KEVIN
We both are. We are the lead detectives.

SGT. JACOBS flashes her badge again.

SGT. JACOBS
Not anymore, you're not. This is now a DEA matter.

KEVIN
This is my crime scene. There are over a half a dozen homicides inside. We have an investigation to ensue.

SGT. JACOBS
Then by all means, call your meat wagon, scoop up their remains, and do your thing. But any witnesses, any evidence, or anything to do with my investigation will be confiscated.

PATRICK
Wait a minute. What do you mean your investigation?

SGT. JACOBS
We've had undercover agents on the inside for over a year now. And I would appreciate it if you would show my agents some professional courtesy.

SGT. JACOBS points over to the SQUAD CAR.

SGT. JACOBS (CONT'D)
Release my agents, now!

KEVIN
WHAT?

PATRICK
You have to be shitting me.

SGT. JACOBS
I am not shitting you.

KEVIN calls over a nearby POLICE OFFICER.

KEVIN
Officer, would you please release those two suspects.
(sarcastically)
Apparently they are DEA.

The OFFICER walks over to the SQUAD CAR and opens the door. He helps them BOTH out and takes off their handcuffs.

MAGGIE and JUSTINE rub their wrists. SGT. JACOBS, KEVIN, and PATRICK walk over.

SGT. JACOBS
You two all right?

MAGGIE
Fine, Sarge.

JUSTINE
Me, too.

KEVIN
(angry)
You're an undercover DEA agent? Were you ever going to tell me or were you just using me for information?

JUSTINE
Kevin I . . .

KEVIN interrupts.

KEVIN
You lied to me. We are all suppose to be on the same team. I never wanna see you again.
(disgusted)
I'm out of here.

KEVIN walks away. PATRICK looks at MAGGIE, disappointingly, and follows behind KEVIN.

MAGGIE
Patrick, wait.

SGT. JACOBS turns to her FIELD AGENTS.

SGT. JACOBS
All right, people, lock it down.

The FIELD AGENTS hit the crime scene.

SGT. JACOBS (CONT'D)
(to Justine and Maggie)
You two, over here.

MAGGIE and JUSTINE are preoccupied with KEVIN and PATRICK.

SGT. JACOBS (CONT'D)
Hey, you two get your heads in the game. Don't worry about them and listen up.

She leans in to the TWO.

SGT. JACOBS (CONT'D)
With some stroke of luck, the heavens have smiled upon us. Mac has come out of his coma.

JUSTINE
(eyes widen)
WHAT? Are you sure?

SGT. JACOBS
Got word about an hour ago. I was going to pull you two out of here until this mess happened. Damn Russians.

JUSTINE
Maggie and I secured evidence. We have Slim's logs and lap top. I put them inside the beer cooler behind the main bar.

SGT. JACOBS
Good work. We have G.o.n.y. by the balls now. But we have to move quickly. With your evidence and Mac's testimony, we can close this case. This is the big one, ladies. This is the kind of bust that careers are made of.

JUSTINE
Let's do it. Come on.

MAGGIE
I'm ready.

SGT. JACOBS
Meet me at the hospital in two hours. Let them prep Mac for relocation so we can move him to a safe house. Keep it quiet. If G.o.n.y. catches wind of this, there will be a price on Mac's head so fast. Understood?

JUSTINE
Two hours. Got it.

MAGGIE

Yes, Sarge.

SGT. JACOBS

You two get out of here and go clean up. I'll secure the evidence and handle the rest of the red tape.

MAGGIE and JUSTINE head (O.S).

SGT. JACOBS heads for the entrance to the LION's DEN to secure JUSTINE and MAGGIE's evidence hidden inside the beer cooler. She passes through the crime scene.

KEVIN looks over at her. The TWO stare at each other for a moment. SGT. JACOBS gives him a smirk of power and enters inside the LION's DEN.

KEVIN begins to act peculiar. He scans the area and then looks towards a POLICE OFFICER and his SQUAD CAR.

P.O.V. KEVIN:

He sees SLIM in the back of the SQUAD CAR.

KEVIN

(to Patrick)

I'll be right back.

PATRICK

Okay.

KEVIN walks towards a POLICE OFFICER and his SQUAD CAR. He quickly peers over his shoulder.

P.O.V. KEVIN:

He sees PATRICK interacting with some POLICE OFFICERS.

KEVIN

Officer.

POLICE OFFICER

Yes, sir.

KEVIN

I'm taking the prisoner in for questioning.

POLICE OFFICER
Okay, sir.

The POLICE OFFICER moves aside. KEVIN opens the door and pulls SLIM out.

KEVIN
Come on. Let's move, scumbag.

SLIM moves out quickly. KEVIN walks him to his UNMARKED CAR.

PATRICK happens to look over and sees KEVIN with SLIM in his custody. KEVIN opens the door and pushes SLIM inside. He moves swiftly to the driver's seat, starts the car, and drives off.

PATRICK
What the hell?

PATRICK starts to follows after him. But KEVIN drives off in a haste. PATRICK makes his way to the POLICE OFFICER.

PATRICK (CONT'D)
Hey, where did Detective Malley take Slim?

POLICE OFFICER
He said he was taking him in for questioning.

PATRICK
Really?

POLICE OFFICER
That's what he said.

SGT. JACOBS walks over to PATRICK with the EVIDENCE secured under her arm.

SGT. JACOBS
Excuse me, detective.

PATRICK turns around.

PATRICK
Yes, Agent Jacobs.

SGT. JACOBS
They need one of you inside right away.

PATRICK looks back in KEVIN's direction then at SGT. JACOBS.

PATRICK
I guess that would be me.
(beat)
Thanks.

PATRICK walks away towards the entrance to the LION's DEN.

SGT. JACOBS
You're welcome.

SGT. JACOBS watches him for a minute then walks away with the EVIDENCE in hand.

Her CELL PHONE rings. She answers it.

SGT. JACOBS (CONT'D)
Jacobs.
(looks at the evidence)
Yes, everything's in motion. We have two hours.

TIME CUT TO:

INT. JUSTINE'S APT. -- LATER

MAGGIE is fresh out of the shower, still in a towel. JUSTINE is fully dressed.

JUSTINE's cell phone rings. She looks down at the caller id.

JUSTINE
(to Maggie)
It's Kevin.

She answers it.

JUSTINE (CONT'D)
Kevin. Where have you been? I called you five times.
(beat)
I'm sorry too. Okay. No, it's not a problem.

JUSTINE hangs up her cell phone.

JUSTINE (CONT'D)
(to Maggie)
That was Kevin. He wants to talk. I'm going to his apartment.

MAGGIE
Are you sure? What about the hospital?

JUSTINE
We still have time. I'll meet you and Sarge there.

JUSTINE grabs her keys and pocket book.

MAGGIE
How am I supposed to get there?

JUSTINE
Call a cab. Tell them what hospital. Room 407. I'll meet you there.

MAGGIE
Where's Patrick? Is he with Kevin?

JUSTINE
He didn't say. Just call him. I'll see you at the hospital.

JUSTINE rushes out and slams the door behind her.

CUT TO:

INT. NYPD POLICE PRECINCT - LATER

PATRICK walks through the door and walks up to the front desk. A DESK OFFICER sits behind the desk.

PATRICK
(to the desk officer)
Did Detective Malley come through here with a suspect?

DESK OFFICER
No. Haven't seen him. It's been quiet.

PATRICK turns and heads back out the front door.

PATRICK
(to himself)
What the hell's going on?

CUT TO:

EXT. KEVIN'S APT. -- HALLWAY -- LATER

JUSTINE knocks on the door. She waits. KEVIN opens the door, half dressed.

KEVIN
Come in.

KEVIN enters and JUSTINE follows behind him. She closes the door, but the door doesn't close all the way. She doesn't realize it and continues to follow behind KEVIN.

INT. KEVIN'S APT. - CONTINUOUS

KEVIN's Apartment is spacious. It is decorated very well in a modern art Deco decor. A huge LIBRARY makes up the back wall of his apartment.

KEVIN
I was just about to jump in the shower. Then I thought we could go for a walk.

JUSTINE
I'd like that. But we have to make it fast. Duty calls.

KEVIN
Oh . . . right. Give me five minutes.

KEVIN walks into the bedroom.

P.O.V. JUSTINE:

She sees a BOOK on KEVIN's COFFEE TABLE still wrapped in cellophane.

The TITLE reads: "*THE GHOST AND THE DARKNESS.*"

JUSTINE
New book?

KEVIN (O.S.)
Just arrived today. Limited edition. It's about the two lions in Africa that attacked the railroad workers.

JUSTINE
I know. Saw the movie. Val Kilmer and Michael Douglas.

KEVIN
Right.

WE HEAR THE SHOWER TURN ON.

JUSTINE saunters over to KEVIN's LIBRARY and begins to scan through the various titles.

The more she scans, the more peculiar the titles become.

JUSTINE
You sure have a lot of ghost stories.

KEVIN (O.S.)
What's that?

JUSTINE
Nothing.
(to herself)
A lot of stories with the word ghost in it.

P.O.V. JUSTINE:

She scans through the various titles. "*GHOST OF MISSISSIPPI,*" "*GHOST RIDER,*" "*GHOST IN MY CLOSET.*" She finally stops at "*CASPER THE FRIENDLY GHOST.*"

JUSTINE (O.S.)
Isn't that cute.

She removes the book from the shelf. She accidentally drops it.

JUSTINE (O.S.) (CONT'D)
What's that?

She sees a HUNDRED DOLLAR BILL sticking out of the top of the book.

She kneels down to pick it up. She opens the book to find the middle of the book is hollowed out. Inside the hollowed middle is numerous HUNDRED DOLLAR BILLS.

JUSTINE (O.S.) (CONT'D)
What the hell?

She pushes the money back inside and puts the book back on the shelf.

She then begins to pull out any BOOK with "GHOST" in the title.

BOOK after BOOK is revealed with hollowed middles with MONEY hidden inside. She drops them all to the floor.

Piles of BOOKS and MONEY lay by her feet.

A nervousness feeling overcomes her.

She moves to the coffee table and rips the cellophane off of his new book. She finds more MONEY and a PLANE TICKET.

WE HEAR THE SHOWER TURN OFF.

Her eyes look up towards the bathroom.

CUT TO:

INT. PATRICK'S CAR -- MOVING - MOMENTS LATER

PATRICK drives through traffic. He dials his cell phone. He puts it to his ear and waits. He then angrily hangs up.

PATRICK
(to himself)
What's going on, Kevin? Why did you turn off your phone?

BACK TO:

INT. KEVIN'S APT. - CONTINUOUS

KEVIN walks out of his bedroom, dressed. He fixes the buttons on his sleeves.

KEVIN
Come on, Justine, let's get out of here . . .

He stops in his tracks.

JUSTINE sits on his couch. Her legs crossed. KEVIN's new book fanned open across her lap as if she were reading it. KEVIN can see the other BOOKS and MONEY spread out on the floor.

JUSTINE
Good book, but I definitely liked the movie better.

KEVIN grows nervous.

KEVIN
Hold on, Justine. There is an explanation.

JUSTINE
What, the banks aren't safe enough? Or is it this is the kind of income you can't claim so you have to hide it?

KEVIN
Don't you dare lecture me about secrets. You just unloaded a huge secret on me today, now didn't you?

JUSTINE
Don't you dare throw that in my face, not now. You told me your parents were rich. That's how you could afford this place. You're a fucking liar.

JUSTINE tosses the PLANE TICKET out from behind the book.

JUSTINE (CONT'D)
What's with the one-way ticket to the Caribbean? Don't plan on coming back?

KEVIN
Listen . . .

JUSTINE interrupts.

JUSTINE
How long has it been, Kevin?

KEVIN
How long has what been?

JUSTINE

How long have you been selling drugs and killing people?

(beat)

Long enough to build a library?

KEVIN

What are you talking about?

JUSTINE

How long have you been G.o.n.y?

KEVIN

What?

JUSTINE

The fucking Ghost of New York, Kevin. You seem to forget I am an agent. All signs point to you.

KEVIN begins to laugh. A hard evil laugh deep from within his stomach.

KEVIN

You will never know the answer to that question.

ANGLE ON:

KEVIN slowly reaches around his waist towards his back. There is a GUN tucked into his belt.

JUSTINE

So all your investigations, all your evidence, it was you all along that sabotaged the crime scenes, just to protect yourself and your goons! How do you live with yourself?

KEVIN

Quite easily! It's called millions of dollars.

(angry)

Do you think I want to live with these homicides for the rest of my life? Day in and day out. Each one imbedded in my mind. The nightmares, the sleepless nights.

(sincerely)

I refuse to be surrounded by death for the rest of my life. REFUSE!

JUSTINE
So that's how you justify your actions? Kill to get rich?

KEVIN
You're damn right. People do it every day for nothing. Why not profit from it?

JUSTINE
And how long has Patrick been involved?

KEVIN
My dear, Patrick, the poor sap, is oblivious, just like you. And just to clear the airways, sweetheart, I knew you, Maggie, and Mac were agents. But it all ends tonight. You dug too deep and now you need to be buried.

KEVIN grabs his gun from his belt and points it at JUSTINE.

WE HEAR A CELL PHONE RING.

FADE TO BLACK:

WE HEAR TWO GUNSHOTS FIRE OVER THE BLACK SCREEN.

FADE BACK IN:

INT. JUSTINE'S APT. - LATER

MAGGIE hangs up her cell phone, angry.

MAGGIE
(angry)
Fine, Patrick. I tried.

MAGGIE tosses her cell phone onto the couch in disgust.

MAGGIE (CONT'D)
You don't want to talk to me, I don't want to talk to you.

She grabs her pocketbook and leaves the apartment. Her cell phone still on the couch.

DISSOLVE TO:

EXT. HOSPITAL - LATER

MAGGIE exits a TAXI CAB. She hands the CABBIE her fare.

MAGGIE
Thank you. Keep the change.

The TAXI CAB drives away. MAGGIE makes her way into the Hospital.

CUT TO:

INT. HOSPITAL -- HALLWAY -- MOVING -- MOMENTS LATER

The 4th floor of the Hospital is quiet. Not a lot of activity

ANGLE ON:

The wheels of a GURNEY move forward with an eerie squeak.

CAMERA PANS up to REVEAL SLIM. He pushes the empty gurney disguised in a full hospital UNIFORM. He even has a fake I.D. BADGE hooked to his shirt.

He wheels the gurney past a STATION NURSE. She sits behind her desk engrossed in her activities. She doesn't pay any attention to him.

SLIM makes his way down the hallway towards a POLICE OFFICER dressed in a suit.

The POLICE OFFICER stands in front of room 407.

SLIM saunters past the POLICE OFFICER with a head gesture. The POLICE OFFICER gestures back. SLIM can see his BADGE hooked to his belt.

SLIM
Evening, officer.

POLICE OFFICER
Evening.

SLIM walks down two rooms and stops.

SLIM
Excuse me, officer. Can you assist me for one second?

The POLICE OFFICER walks over kindly.

POLICE OFFICER
No problem. What do you need?

SLIM
If you can just help me through that door. That would be great.

The POLICE OFFICER turns his back to SLIM and reaches for the handle of the door. SLIM removes a silenced pistol from under the sheets of the gurney and plants TWO SHOTS between the POLICE OFFICER's bulletproof vest and into his side. The POLICE OFFICER wrenches in pain and falls back onto the gurney. SLIM is quick. He maneuvers the POLICE OFFICER entirely onto the gurney and covers his body with the gurney sheet.

He rolls the gurney into the room and closes the door. He surveys the area to make sure all is clear.

He snakes his way towards the fourth floor stairwell and exits through the door.

CUT TO:

INT. HOSPITAL STAIRWELL - CONTINUOUS

SLIM
(whispers)
All clear, boss.

G.O.N.Y. emerges from the shadows of the stairwell. He is in full disguise.

SLIM (CONT'D)
We are all clear. Just one nurse. Did you take care of the security room?

G.O.N.Y. (Voice Box)
All taken care of.

SMASH CUT TO:

INT. HOSPITAL SECURITY ROOM - MOMENTS LATER

TWO SECURITY GUARDS lay dead inside with their throats cut. One GUARD lays on the floor and the other lays across his blood-soaked desk.

The SECURITY MONITORS for the hospital are all SNOW.

BACK TO:

INT. STAIRWELL - CONTINUOUS

SLIM
All right. All the loose ends are almost tied up. Just one more to go.

G.O.N.Y. (Voice Box)
Actually, there are two.

SLIM
Huh?

G.O.N.Y quickly thrusts a KNIFE upwards from behind his back. It slams into SLIM's throat. He grabs SLIM by his neck, pulls the KNIFE out, and throws SLIM violently down the stairwell.

SLIM tumbles viciously down the stairs and lands hard at the bottom.

G.O.N.Y. (Voice Box)
Now there's one more.

G.O.N.Y. exits the stairwell and enters the hospital hallway.

INT. HOSPITAL-- HALLWAY -- MOMENTS LATER

He moves like a cat and enters room 407. Just as G.O.N.Y. closes the room door, MAGGIE exits the hospital elevator.

She makes her way over to the NURSE and flashes her badge.

MAGGIE
I am here for a patient in room 407.

NURSE
Sure, officer. No problem. It's down the hallway. You can't miss it.

MAGGIE glances down the hallway. She doesn't see a GUARD.

MAGGIE

Isn't there supposed to be a guard at the door?

NURSE

He was just there a minute ago. Maybe he went to get a cup of coffee or use the restroom.

MAGGIE

Anybody else been through here? Other police officers?

NURSE shakes her head.

NURSE

An orderly passed by before. But they're in and out all night. As far as police, just you so far.

MAGGIE looks down at her watch.

MAGGIE

Okay, thanks.

NURSE

You're welcome.

MAGGIE makes her way down the hallway. She stands in front of the door for a moment. She looks around and then looks down at her watch again.

She enters the room.

INT. ROOM 407 - CONTINUOUS

The room is dark. A BLUE CURTAIN separates the room into two halves. The sounds of the hospital machines give the room some life.

MAGGIE looks at MAC from a distance. He lays there, peacefully asleep. She moves slowly towards his bed to give him a better look.

She positions herself on the right side of the BLUE CURTAIN.

MAGGIE

(whispers)

And you must be Mac.

She leans over his bed.

MAGGIE (CONT'D)
(whispers)
I guess you're going to end this mess.

P.O.V. MAGGIE:

She leans in closer and notices a TATTOO on MAC's RIGHT FOREARM.

MAGGIE (O.S.)
Wait a minute.

CLOSE UP.

The TATTOO is of a CELTIC CROSS. There is writing on it which reads: *"IN LOVING MEMORY OF SEAN O'BRIAN."*

MAGGIE (O.S.) (CONT'D)
What the hell?

MAGGIE steps away from the bed, confused. She nears the BLUE CURTAIN.

ANGLE ON:

The BLUE CURTAIN behind MAGGIE begins to move. G.O.N.Y.'s HAND protrudes through the break of the curtain.

In his hand is a NEEDLE. He violently plunges it into MAGGIE's left shoulder.

MAGGIE shrieks with pain and surprise. She stumbles over the end of MAC's bed and falls to the floor.

G.O.N.Y. fully emerges from behind the BLUE CURTAIN.

G.O.N.Y. (Voice Box)
Hello, my dear.

MAGGIE rolls around on the floor. Her vision and judgment become blurred.

P.O.V. MAGGIE:

G.O.N.Y.'s face and body distort in her vision. He looks like an absolute monster.

MAGGIE (O.S.)
What the hell's going on?

MAGGIE scampers. She tries to remove her gun from her holster. She drops it to the floor in her frantic state. G.O.N.Y. is quick to respond. He reaches down and picks it up.

G.O.N.Y. (Voice Box)
You won't be needing that.

He tucks it into his belt.

G.O.N.Y. (Voice Box) (CONT'D)
Settle down, my dear. I am not here to hurt you.

MAGGIE
Who are you?

G.O.N.Y. (Voice Box)
Oh, I think you know who I am.

MAGGIE
G.O.N.Y.?

G.O.N.Y. puts a finger over his mouth.

G.O.N.Y. (Voice Box)
Shhh . . . don't tell anybody.
(beat)
The Ghost of New York now stands before you. And I stand before you with a gift. A gift that's been driving you. A gift you've been searching for.

MAGGIE crawls towards a chair next to MAC's bed. She pulls herself up and sits in the chair.

G.O.N.Y. (Voice Box) (CONT'D)
There you go. Sit down and have a seat.

MAGGIE
What did you give me?

G.O.N.Y. holds up the NEEDLE.

G.O.N.Y. (Voice Box)
Just a little concoction I conjured up.

He tosses the empty NEEDLE onto MAC's bed. He stands over MAGGIE with his dominance. MAGGIE's state of mind becomes solemn and controllable.

G.O.N.Y. (Voice Box) (CONT'D)
We have much to talk about.

MAGGIE's head slumps from the drug.

MAGGIE
What could we possibly have to talk about?

G.O.N.Y. (Voice Box)
Everything.
(points to Mac)
For starters, him.

MAGGIE
I don't even know him.

G.O.N.Y. (Voice Box)
On the contrary, my dear, you know him very well. John MacDaniels legally changed his name years ago. John MacDaniels use to be Thomas Macallister.

MAGGIE raise her head up.

MAGGIE
What?

G.O.N.Y. (Voice Box)
I thought that might get your attention.
(beat)
I knew Mac here wasn't dead. But I needed a way inside. If Slim didn't call Mac up to the penthouse that night, I wouldn't be in this predicament.
(beat)
So I had to think of a way to clean up this mess. A way so clever that no fingers would point to me. So I dug deep and found a little red-headed girl from Chicago with a history.

MAGGIE turns and looks at MAC. She tightens her fists. The drug influencing her. G..O.N.Y.'s voice box voice hypnotizing her every thought.

G.O.N.Y. (Voice Box) (CONT'D)
Yes, Maggie.
(beat)
Your brother's killer is here before you. Right in front of your eyes. He is here for the taking. All those years. All those tears.
(beat)
Your vengeance is staring you right in the face. A gift to you, given by me.

MAGGIE stands up out of the chair. Her heart pumping. Her mind racing.

G.O.N.Y. removes the same KNIFE he used on SLIM and the SECURITY GUARDS.

G.O.N.Y. (Voice Box) (CONT'D)
Here, Maggie. Use my knife. Cut his throat from ear to ear. Make him pay for the pain you suffered.

G.O.N.Y. slowly hands the KNIFE over to MAGGIE. MAGGIE is so mind-controlled she takes it.

G.O.N.Y. (Voice Box) (CONT'D)
There you go, girl. Cut his throat.

She moves over MAC and places the KNIFE underneath MAC's throat. Her hand trembles and shakes. The blade ready to cut. But she fights. She fights the drug inside her. She remembers what JUSTINE had told her when she took the ecstasy.

JUSTINE's VOICE echoes inside her head.

JUSTINE (V.O.)
Don't ever forget the side you are on. You are a cop and they are the criminals. Learn to maintain and never let the drug affect your actions. Overcome it and use it. Learn to focus under pressure.

MAGGIE closes her eyes and tries to fight the drug. She lowers the KNIFE away from MAC's throat.

G.O.N.Y. (Voice Box)
What are you doing? Take your revenge!

MAGGIE tosses the KNIFE onto the floor.

MAGGIE
NO. I am no murderer.

MAGGIE begins to regain some focus. She looks at G.O.N.Y. Then something catches her eye.

P.O.V. MAGGIE:

She peers down and notices G.O.N.Y. has on WHITE SNEAKERS. Familiar WHITE SNEAKERS.

MAGGIE
What's the matter, sarge, feet hurt?

G.O.N.Y. (Voice Box)
Clever girl.

Suddenly, MAC raises up from behind G.O.N.Y. With all the strength he can muster, he wraps his arms around G.O.N.Y.'s head and pulls off his MASK.

MAC
(loudly)
YOU BITCH!

WE REVEAL SGT.JACOBS AS G.O.N.Y.

The MASK flies off and the VOICE BOX smashes to the ground. SGT. JACOBS grabs MAGGIE's GUN from her waist and bashes MAC in the face. MAC falls out of his hospital bed onto the other side of the room.

MAGGIE tries to rush in, but SGT. JACOBS is quick. She turns the gun on MAGGIE and cocks back the hammer. MAGGIE pauses in her movement.

SGT. JACOBS
Don't move!
(beat)
You are a clever little bitch. I will give you that.

MAGGIE
I guess our evidence never made it to your office?

SGT. JACOBS
That's the least of your worries.

MAGGIE

Why? Why me?

SGT. JACOBS

(laughs)

Because, when you found out who Mac really was you went insane. You killed Slim, the security guards, and then Mac. I tried to stop you, but you were all whacked out on some sort of drug.

MAGGIE

That will never stick.

SGT. JACOBS

I believe I have you on record taking ecstasy and your little nights out on the town, drinking. I have motive, and that's all I need to make it stick.

MAGGIE

That's why I was called to New York in such a hurry. It was you.

(beat)

Justine will never go along with you.

SGT. JACOBS

My dear, Justine is no longer with us.

SGT. JACOBS raises MAGGIE's gun.

Suddenly, the NURSE bursts through the door.

NURSE

What's going on in here?

SGT. JACOBS turns towards the door for a second. It gives MAGGIE an opening. MAGGIE rushes her.

SGT. JACOBS turns around. MAGGIE grabs the gun and wrestles with SGT. JACOBS. MAGGIE pushes her wrist up towards the ceiling. The gun fires.

The NURSE runs out of the room scared to death. The door stays open.

The TWO struggle. SGT. JACOBS spins MAGGIE around and kicks her hard in the stomach. MAGGIE slides into the hallway. She jumps up onto her feet quickly.

INT. HOSPITAL-- HALLWAY - CONTINUOUS

SGT. JACOBS comes out of the room, weapon hot. MAGGIE ducks to the left of the door and grabs the gun again as SGT. JACOBS's exits. MAGGIE struggles a bit and then nails SGT. JACOBS with a kick of her own. The gun comes loose and falls to the floor.

SGT. JACOBS is tough. She shakes off the kick. Maggie rushes back at her and attempts another kick. SGT. JACOBS blocks the kick and nails MAGGIE square in the jaw with a powerful punch. MAGGIE slides to the ground, hurt.

SGT. JACOBS reaches down and grabs the gun. She moves towards MAGGIE and hovers over her. She aims the gun at MAGGIE's head, ready to fire.

Suddenly, a GUN presses against SGT. JACOBS's head and a familiar voice calls out.

JUSTINE (O.S.)

Don't move.

CAMERA PULLS OUT to REVEAL JUSTINE and PATRICK. PATRICK's right shoulder bleeds from an apparent bullet wound.

FLASHBACK TO:

INT. KEVIN'S APT. - EVENING

KEVIN grabs his gun from his belt.

WE HEAR A CELL PHONE RING.

KEVIN turns around to SEE PATRICK. PATRICK's CELL PHONE RINGS again from inside his jacket, giving him away.

KEVIN fires a shot that hits PATRICK in the right shoulder. PATRICK falls to the ground.

KEVIN turns to fire at JUSTINE. A bullet fires through the book on her lap and hits KEVIN right in the head. KEVIN falls backwards onto the floor.

JUSTINE drops the book to REVEAL a gun she had hidden behind the book on her lap.

She quickly jumps up.

JUSTINE
PATRICK.

BACK TO:

INT. HOSPITAL-- HALLWAY - CONTINUOUS

JUSTINE has SGT. JACOBS on the floor. She handcuffs her.

PATRICK is kneeling down next to MAGGIE. He holds her.

CAMERA PULLS AWAY.

FADE TO BLACK:

MAGGIE (V.O.)
Never in my wildest dreams would I have thought I would meet Tommy Macallister again.

FADE BACK IN:

WE SEE MAGGIE sit bedside JOHN MACDANIELS a.k.a. TOMMY MACALLISTER.

He talks to MAGGIE from his hospital bed.

WE DON'T HEAR HIS WORDS.

MAGGIE (V.O.) (CONT'D)
He explained to me that he loved my brother. That they kept their relationship a secret from Mike Mahoney.
(beat)
He told me Sean was hurting from the relationship with my father. He used the drugs to escape. He told me that the night Sean died he thought Sean wasn't in his right state of mind. That he talked about suicide constantly. That Sean killed himself purposely with the overdose.
(beat)
I listened, but I didn't want to believe him. After my brother's death, he wanted to change. He left Chicago and changed his name. He wanted to forget his past.

He never wanted to feel that pain again.
(beat)
I told him all about me and my reasoning for becoming an agent. He vowed to me that he would help me reach that goal. In my brother's memory. Fifty-two criminals in my brother's name.

WE SEE MAGGIE AND JOHN MACDANIELS HUG.

DISSOLVE TO:

EXT. NYC COURTHOUSE - MORNING

MAGGIE, JUSTINE and PATRICK stand by the Courthouse steps. PATRICK has his arm in a sling.

PEOPLE mill about.

NEWS CREWs circle the area, ready for their story.

A GAGGLE of NYPD POLICE OFFICERs exit a POLICE VAN.

NEWS CREWS flutter towards the POLICE OFFICERs.

ANGLE ON:

SGT. JACOBS exits the POLICE VAN and walks in the custody of the POLICE OFFICERs. She wears an ORANGE JUMPSUIT and is handcuffed and shackled. The POLICE OFFICERs escort her into the Courthouse. She walks with her head down in shame.

JUSTINE
(to Maggie)
How does it feel to finally put away number fifty-two?

MAGGIE looks at PATRICK. PATRICK reaches out his hand. MAGGIE takes it.

MAGGIE
It feels good. Really good.

The THREE begin their walk up the steps.

CAMERA PULLS OUT.

DISSOLVE TO:

EXT. KEYSTONE PUB AND GRILL - AFTERNOON

MAGGIE (V.O.)
The Ghost of New York was finally revealed. And we did get number fifty-two. Sgt. Serina Jacobs got three consecutive life sentences with no chance of parole.
(beat)
After the trial, I had to relax. Justine stayed in New York with Mac, and I brought Patrick home to meet my family.

WE SEE BRIAN crash through the front door of the pub. He lands on his back into a pile of snow. He looks up at the door with a smile.

BRIAN
I missed you, too, sis!

CAMERA PANS UP into the sky.

FADE TO BLACK:

END CREDITS.

"*MAGGIE MAY,*" performed by "*ROD STEWART,*" plays.

www.ingramcontent.com/pod-product-compliance
Lightning Source LLC
Chambersburg PA
CBHW060606310726
48982CB00008B/1255/J

* 9 7 8 1 7 3 5 1 0 1 7 0 5 *